George Gordon Byron

Selections from the works of Lord Byron

George Gordon Byron

Selections from the works of Lord Byron

ISBN/EAN: 9783743338340

Manufactured in Europe, USA, Canada, Australia, Japa

Cover: Foto ©Andreas Hilbeck / pixelio.de

Manufactured and distributed by brebook publishing software
(www.brebook.com)

George Gordon Byron

Selections from the works of Lord Byron

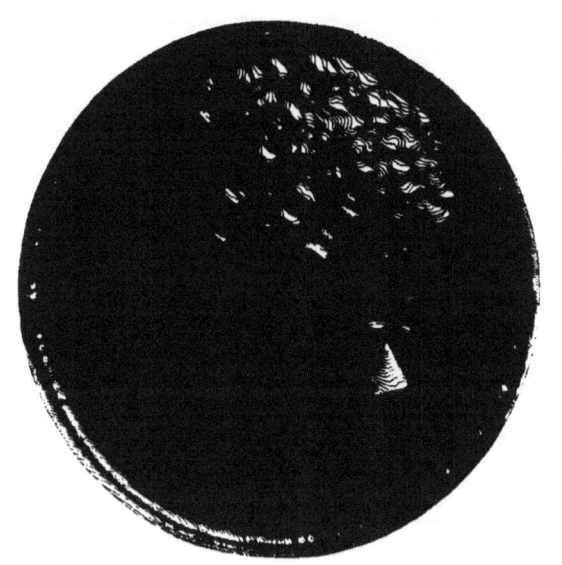

MOXON'S MINIATURE POETS.

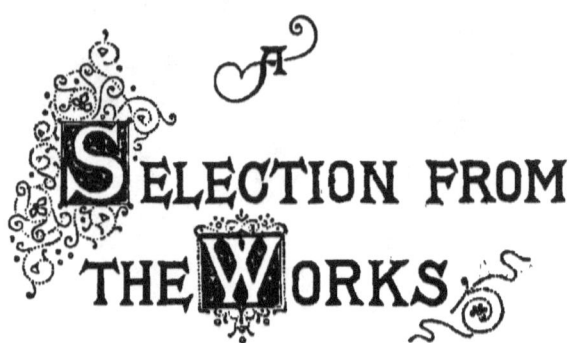

A SELECTION FROM THE WORKS

OF

LORD BYRON.

EDITED AND PREFACED BY ALGERNON CHAS. SWINBURNE.

LONDON:
EDWARD MOXON & CO., DOVER STREET.
1866.

THE COVER FROM A DESIGN BY JOHN LEIGHTON, F.S.A.;
THE SELECTION MADE BY THE KIND PERMISSION OF JOHN MURRAY;
THE SERIES PROJECTED AND SUPERINTENDED BY

PREFACE.

THE most delicate and thoughtful of English critics
has charged the present generation of Englishmen
with forgetfulness of Byron.   It is not a light charge :
and it is not ungrounded.   Men born when this
century was getting into its forties were baptized into
another church than his with the rites of another
creed.   Upon their ears, first after the cadences of
elder poets, fell the faultless and fervent melodies
of Tennyson.   To them, chief among the past heroes
of the younger century, three men appeared as pre-
dominant in poetry; Coleridge, Keats, and Shelley.
Behind these were effaced, on either hand, the two
great opposing figures of Byron and Wordsworth.
No man under twenty can just now be expected to
appreciate these.   The time was when all boys and
girls who paddled in rhyme and dabbled in sentiment
were wont to adore the presence or the memory of

Byron with foolish faces of praise. It is of little moment to him or to us that they have long since ceased to cackle and begun to hiss. They have become used to better verse and carefuller workmen ; and must be forgiven if after such training they cannot at once appreciate the splendid and imperishable excellence which covers all his offences and outweighs all his defects : the excellence of sincerity and strength. Without these no poet can live ; but few have ever had so much of them as Byron. His sincerity indeed is difficult to discover and define; but it does in effect lie at the root of all his good works : deformed by pretension and defaced by assumption, masked by folly and veiled by affectation ; but perceptible after all, and priceless.

It is no part of my present office to rewrite the history of a life in which every date and event that could be given would now seem trite and stale to all possible readers. If, after so many promises and hints, something at once new and true shall at length be unearthed or extricated, which may affect for the better or the worse our judgment of the man, it will be possible and necessary to rewrite it. Meantime this among other chances "lies on the lap of the gods ;" and especially on the lap of a goddess who still treads our earth. Until she speaks, we cannot

guess what she may have to say ; and can only pass
by with reverent or with sceptical reticence.

Thus much however we may safely assert : that no
man's work was ever more influenced by his character ; and that no man's character was ever more
influenced by his circumstances.   Rather from things
without than from things within him did the spirit
of Byron assume colour and shape.   His noblest verse
leapt on a sudden into life after the heaviest evils had
fallen upon him which even he ever underwent.
From the beginning indeed he had much to fight
against : and three impediments hung about him at
starting, the least of which would have weighed down
a less strong man : youth, and genius, and an
ancient name.   In spite of all three he made his way ;
and suffered for it.   At the first chance given or
taken, every obscure and obscene thing that lurks for
pay or prey among the fouler shallows and thickets
of literature flew against him ; every hound and every
hireling lavished upon him the loathsome tribute of
their abuse ; all nameless creatures that nibble and
prowl, upon whom the serpent's curse has fallen, to
go upon his belly and eat dust all the days of his life,
assailed him with their foulest venom and their
keenest fangs.   And the promise given of old to their
kind was now at least fulfilled ; they did bruise his

heel. · But the heads of such creatures are so small
that it is hard to bruise them in return ; it would first
be necessary to discern them.

That Byron was able to disregard and to outlive
the bark and the bite of such curs as these is small
praise enough : the man who cannot do as much is
destructible, and therefore contemptible. He did
far more than this ; he withstood the weight of circumstances to the end ; not always without complaint,
but always without misgiving. His glorious courage,
his excellent contempt for things contemptible, and
hatred of hateful men, are enough of themselves to
embalm and endear his memory in the eyes of all
who are worthy to pass judgment upon him. And
these qualities gave much of their own value to verse
not otherwise or not always praiseworthy. Even at
its best, the serious poetry of Byron is often so rough
and loose, so weak in the screws and joints which
hold together the framework of verse, that it is not
easy to praise it enough without seeming to condone
or to extenuate such faults as should not be over-
looked or forgiven. No poet is so badly represented
by a book of selections. It must show something of
his weakness ; it cannot show all of his strength.
Often, after a noble overture, the last note struck
is either dissonant or ineffectual. His magnificent

masterpiece, which must endure for ever among the precious relics of the world, will not bear dissection or extraction. The merit of "Don Juan" does not lie in any part, but in the whole. There is in that great poem an especial and exquisite balance and sustenance of alternate tones which cannot be expressed or explained by the utmost ingenuity of selection. Haidée is supplanted by Dudu, the shipwreck by the siege, the Russian court by the English household; and this perpetual change, this tidal variety of experience and emotion, gives to the poem something of the breadth and freshness of the sea. Much of the poet's earlier work is or seems unconsciously dishonest; this, if not always or wholly unaffected, is as honest as the sunlight, as frank as the sea-wind. Here, and here alone, the student of his work may recognize and enjoy the ebb and flow of actual life. Here the pulse of vital blood may be felt in tangible flesh. Here for the first time the style of Byron is beyond all praise or blame: a style at once swift and supple, light and strong, various and radiant. Between "Childe Harold" and "Don Juan" the same difference exists which a swimmer feels between lake-water and sea-water; the one is fluent, yielding, invariable; the other has in it a life and pulse, a sting and a swell, which touch and excite

the nerves like fire or like music. Across the stanzas
of " Don Juan " we swim forward as over " the broad
backs of the sea"; they break and glitter, hiss and
laugh, murmur and move, like waves that sound or
that subside. There is in them a delicious resistance,
an elastic motion, which salt water has and fresh
water has not. There is about them a wide whole-
some air, full of vivid light and constant wind, which
is only felt at sea. Life undulates and death palpi-
tates in the splendid verse which resumes the evidence of a brave and clear-sighted man concerning
life and death. Here, as at sea, there is enough and
too much of fluctuation and intermission ; the ripple
flags and falls in loose and lazy lines : the foam flies
wide of any mark, and the breakers collapse here
and there in sudden ruin and violent failure. But
the violence and weakness of the sea are preferable to
the smooth sound and equable security of a lake : its
buoyant and progressive impulse sustains and propels
those who would sink through weariness in the flat
and placid shallows. There are others whom it
sickens, and others whom it chills ; these will do well
to steer inshore.

It is natural in writing of Byron to slide into
remembrances of what is likest to his verse. His
work and Shelley's, beyond that of all our other poets,

recall or suggest the wide and high things of nature ; the large likeness of the elements; the immeasurable liberty and the stormy strength of waters and winds. They are strongest when they touch upon these ; and it is worth remark how few are the poets of whom this can be said. Here as elsewhere Shakespeare is supreme when it pleased him ; but it pleased him rarely. No poetry of shipwreck and the sea has ever equalled the great scene of " Pericles;" no such note of music was ever struck out of the clash and contention of tempestuous elements. In Milton the sublimity is chiefly of sound ; the majesty of melodies unsurpassed from all time excludes and supplants all other motives of beauty. In the minds of mediæval poets there was no width or depth to receive and contain such emotion. In Spenser, despite his fertile and fluent ingenuity, his subtle and sleepy graces, the effeminacy of colour no less than the monotony of metre makes it hopeless to look for any trace of that passionate sense of power and delight in great outer things of which we speak here. Among later men, Coleridge and Keats used nature mainly as a stimulant or a sedative; Wordsworth as a vegetable fit to shred into his pot and pare down like the outer leaves of a lettuce for didactic and culinary purposes. All these doubtless in their own fashion loved her, for her

beauties, for her uses, for her effects; hardly one for
herself.

Turn now to Byron or to Shelley. These two at least
were not content to play with her skirts and paddle
in her shallows. Their passion is perfect, a fierce and
blind desire which exalts and impels their verse into the
high places of emotion and expression. They feed upon
nature with a holy hunger, follow her with a divine
lust as of gods chasing the daughters of men. Wind
and fire, the cadences of thunder and the clamours of
the sea, gave to them no less of sensual pleasure than
of spiritual sustenance. These things they desired as
others desire music or wine or the beauty of women.
This outward and indifferent nature of things, cruel in
the eyes of all but her lovers, and even in theirs not
loving, became as pliant to their grasp and embrace
as any Clymene or Leucothea to Apollo's. To them
the large motions and the remote beauties of space
were tangible and familiar as flowers. Of this poetry,
where description melts into passion and contemplation takes fire from delight, the highest sample is
Shelley's " Ode to the West Wind." An imperfect
mastery of his materials keeps the best things of Byron
some few degrees below an equal rank. One native
and incurable defect grew up and strengthened side by
side with his noblest qualities : a feeble and faulty

sense of metre. No poet of equal or inferior rank
ever had so bad an ear. His smoother cadences are
often vulgar and facile; his fresher notes are often
incomplete and inharmonious. His verse stumbles and
jingles, stammers and halts, where there is most need
for a swift and even pace of musical sound. The
rough sonorous changes of the songs in "The Deformed Transformed" rise far higher in harmony and
strike far deeper into the memory than the lax easy
lines in which he at first indulged; but they slip too
readily into notes as rude and weak as the rhymeless
tuneless verse in which they are so loosely set, as
in a cheap and casual frame. The magnificent lyric
measures of "Heaven and Earth" are defaced by the
coarse obtrusion of short lines with jagged edges : no
small offence in a writer of verse. Otherwise these
choral scenes are almost as blameless as they are
brilliant. The poet who above others took delight in
the sense of sounding storms and shaken waters could
not but exult over the vision of deluge with all his
strength and breadth of wing. Tempest and rebellion
and the magnificence of anguish were as the natural
food and fire to kindle and sustain his indomitable
and sleepless spirit. The godless martyrdom of rebels;
the passion that cannot redeem ; the Thebaid whose
first hermit was Cain, the Calvary whose first martyr

was Satan ; these, time after time, allured and inspired
him. Here for once this inner and fiery passion of
thought found outer clothing and expression in the ruin
of a world. Both without and within, the subject was
made for him, and lay ready shapen for the strong
impressure of his hand. His love of wide and tempestuous waters fills his work throughout as with the
broad breath of a sea-wind. Even the weakest of his
poems, a thing stillborn and shapeless, is redeemed
and revived by one glorious verse :—

"When the Poles crashed, and water was the world."

This passion and power in dealing with the higher
things of nature, with her large issues and remote
sources, has been bestowed upon Victor Hugo alone
among our contemporaries. He also can pass beyond
the idyllic details of landscape, and put out from
shore into the wide waste places of the sea. And this
of course is the loftiest form of such poetry as deals
with outward nature and depends upon the forms of
things. In Byron the power given by this passion is
more conspicuous through his want of dramatic capa-
city. Except in the lighter and briefer scenes of "Don
Juan," he was never able to bring two speakers face to
face and supply them with the right words. In struc-
ture as in metre his elaborate tragedies are wholly

condemnable; filled as they are in spirit with the overflow of his fiery energy.   Cain and Manfred are properly monologues decorated and set off by some slight
appendage of ornament or explanation.   In the later
and loftier poem there is no difference perceptible,
except in strength and knowledge, between Lucifer
and Cain.   Thus incompetent to handle the mysteries
and varieties of character, Byron turns always with a
fresh delight and a fresh confidence thither where he
feels himself safe and strong.   No part of his nature was
more profound and sincere than the vigorous love of
such inanimate things as were in tune with his own
spirit and senses.   His professions of contempt were
too loud to express it; scorn is brief or silent; anger
alone finds vent in violent iteration and clamorous
appeal.   He had too much of fury and not enough of
contempt; he foams at things and creatures not worth
a glance or a blow.   But when once clear of men and
confronted with elements, he casts the shell of
pretence and drops the veil of habit; then, as in the
last and highest passage of a poem which has suffered
more from praise than any other from dispraise, his
scorn of men caught in the nets of nature and necessity
has no alloy of untruth; his spirit is mingled with the
sea's, and overlooks with a superb delight the ruins
and the prayers of men.

This loftiest passage in " Childe Harold " has been
so often mouthed and mauled by vulgar admiration
that it now can scarcely be relished.   Like a royal
robe worn out, or a royal wine grown sour, it seems
the worse for having been so good.   But in fact,
allowing for one or two slips and blots, we must after
all replace it among the choice and high possessions
of poetry.   After the first there is hardly a weak line ;
many have a wonderful vigour and melody ; and the
deep and glad disdain of the sea for men and the
works of men passes into the verse in music and fills
it with a weighty and sonorous harmony grave and
sweet as the measured voice of heavy remote waves.
No other passage in the fourth canto will bear to be
torn out from the text ; and this one suffers by extraction.   The other three cantos are more loosely built
and less compact of fabric ; but in the first two there
is little to remember or to praise.   Much of the poem
is written throughout in falsetto ; there is a savour in
many places as of something false and histrionic.   This
singular and deep defect, which defaces so much of
Byron's work, seems also to have deformed his personal character, to have given a twist to his enmities
and left a taint upon his friendships.   He was really
somewhat sombre and sad at heart, and it pleased him
to seem sadder than he was.   He was impressible and

susceptible of pleasure, able to command and enjoy it; and of this also it pleased him to make the most in public. But in fact he was neither a Harold nor a Juan; he was better than these in his own way, and assumed their parts and others with a hypocrisy but half insincere. The fault was probably in great part unconscious, and transparent as a child's acting. To the keen eye and cool judgment of Stendhal it was at once perceptible. Byron's letter to him in defence of Scott was doubtless not insincere; yet it is evident that the writer felt himself to be playing a graceful part to advantage. This fretful and petulant appetite for applause, the proper appanage of small poets and lowly aspirants, had in Byron's case to wrestle with the just pride of place and dignity of genius; no man ever had more of these; yet they did not always support him; he fell even into follies and vulgarities unworthy of a meaner name than his. In effect, when his errors were gravest, he erred through humility and not through pride. Pride would have sustained him far above the remarks and reviews of his day, the praise or dispraise of his hour. As it was, he was vulnerable even by creeping things: and at times their small stings left a poison behind which turned his blood. The contagion of their touch infected him; and he strove under its influence to hiss and wound as they.

Here and there in his letters and reflections, in the loose records of his talk and light fragments of his work, the traces of infection are flagrant.

But these defects were only as scars on the skin, superficial and removable; they are past and done with; while all of him that was true and good remains, as it will to all time. Justice cannot be done to it here or now. It is enough if after careful selection as little injustice be done as possible. His few sonnets, unlike Shelley's, are all good; the best is that on Bonnivard, one of his noblest and completest poems. The versified narratives which in their day were so admirable and famous have yielded hardly a stray sheaf to the gleaner. They have enough of vigour and elasticity to keep life in them yet; but once chipped or broken their fabric would crumble and collapse. The finest among them is certainly the "Giaour;" the weakest is probably "Parisina." But in none of these is there even a glimpse of Byron's higher and rarer faculty. All that can be said for them is that they gave tokens of a talent singularly fertile, rapid and vivid; a certain power of action and motion which redeems them from the complete stagnation of dead verses; a command over words and rhymes never of the best and never of the worst. In the "Giaour" indeed there is something of a fiery sincerity which in its successors appears diluted and debased.*

The change began in Byron when he first found out his comic power, and rose at once beyond sight or shot of any rival. His early satires are wholly devoid of humour, wit, or grace; the verse of "Beppo," bright and soft and fluent, is full at once of all. The sweet light music of its few and low notes was perfect as a prelude to the higher harmonies of laughter and tears,

* Remembering the success of these stories we may believe that Byron's contempt for the critical fashions of a time which extolled his worst work was not wholly affected or assumed; and understand how the instincts of opposition and reaction drove him back into that open idolatry of Pope and his school, which he expressed loudly and foolishly enough. Probably at heart he did really prefer Pope to all men. His critical faculty, if I may steal one phrase from a treasury that may well spare me the loan, was "zero, or even a frightful *minus* quantity;" his judgment never worth the expense of a thought or a word. Besides, he had striven to emulate or at least to copy the exquisite manner · of Pope in his satires, and must have seen how great and im- passable a gulf lay between the master and his pupil. This would naturally lead him to over-estimate what he could not attain; the delicate merit, the keen perfection, the equable balance of force and finish, of sense and style, which raised his favourite so high among writers, if they left him somewhat low among poets: and having himself so bad an ear for metre, he may even have imagined that Pope's verse was musical.

b 2

of scorn and passion, which as yet lay silent in the
future. It is mere folly to seek in English or Italian
verse a precedent or a parallel. The scheme of metre
is Byron's alone; no weaker hand than his could ever
bend that bow, or ever will. Even the Italian poets,
working in a language more flexible and ductile than
ours, could never turn their native metre to such uses,
could never handle their national weapon with such
grace and strength. The *terza rima* remains their own,
after all our efforts to adapt it; it bears here only
forced flowers and crude fruits:* but the *ottava rima*
Byron has fairly conquered and wrested from them.
Before the appearance of " Beppo," no one could foresee what a master's hand might make of the instrument; and no one could predict its further use and
its dormant powers before the advent of " Don Juan."
In the " Vision of Judgment " it appears finally per-

---

* I do not of course forget that our own time has produced
two noble poems in this foreign and alien metre; but neither
" Casa Guidi Windows " nor " The Defence of Guenevere " will
suffice to establish its general excellence or fitness. The poets
have done so well because they could do no less; but there may
be at once good material and good workmanship without good
implements. Neither of them has done more to give footing in
England to the metre of their poems than did Byron himself by
his " Prophecy of Dante." They have done better than this;
but this they have not done.

fected; the metre fits the sense as with close and
pliant armour, the perfect panoply of Achilles. A
poem so short and hasty, based on a matter so worthy
of brief contempt and long oblivion as the funeral and
the fate of George III., bears about it at first sight no
great sign or likelihood of life. But this poem which
we have by us stands alone, not in Byron's work only,
but in the work of the world. Satire in earlier times
had changed her rags for robes; Juvenal had clothed
with fire, and Dryden with majesty, that wandering
and bastard Muse. Byron gave her wings to fly with,
above the reach even of these. Others have had as
much of passion and as much of humour; Dryden
had perhaps as much of both combined. But here
and not elsewhere a third quality is apparent; the
sense of a high and clear imagination. The grave
and great burlesque of King George and St. Peter is
relieved and sustained by the figures of Michael and
Satan. These two, confronted and, corresponding as
noon and night, lift and light up the background of
satire, blood-red or black according to the point of
view. Above all, the balance of thought and passion
is admirable; human indignation and divine irony are
alike understood and expressed: the pure and fiery
anger of men at sight of wrongdoing, the tacit
inscrutable derision of heaven. Upon this light and

lofty poém a commentary might be written longer than
the text and less worth reading: but here it shall not
be. Those who read it with the due delight, not too
gravely and not too lightly, will understand more than
can now be set down; those who read it otherwise
will not understand anything. Even these can hardly
fail to admire the vigour and variety of scorn, the
beauty and the bitterness of verse, which raise it
beyond comparison with any other satire. There is
enough and too much of violence and injustice in the
lines on Southey; but it must be remembered that he
was the first to strike, and with an unfair weapon. A
poet by profession, he had assaulted with feeble fury
another poet, not on the fair and open charge of bad
verses, but under the impertinent and irrelevant plea
that his work was an affliction or an offence to religion
and morality—the most susceptible, as the most in-
tangible, among the creatures of metaphor. A man
less irritable and less powerful than Byron might be
forgiven for any reprisals : and the excellence of his
verses justifies their injustice. But that Southey, who
could win and retain for life the love and the praise of
Landor, was capable of conscious baseness or falsity,
Byron himself in sober moments should hardly have
believed. Between official adoration and not less
official horror—between George deified and Byron

denounced—the Laureate's position was grotesque enough. It was almost a good office to pelt him with the names of hireling and apostate; these charges he could reject and refute. The facts were surely sufficient; that, as to religion, his "present Deity" was the paltriest maniac among kings and Cæsars; as to morality, his feelings or his faith obliged him to decry as pernicious the greatest work of his opponent.

Side by side with the growth of his comic and satiric power, the graver genius of Byron increased and flourished. As the tree grew higher it grew shapelier; the branches it put forth on all sides were fairer of leaf and fuller of fruit than its earlier offshoots had promised. But from these hardly a stray bud or twig can be plucked off by way of sample. No detached morsel of "Don Juan," no dismembered fragment of "Cain," will serve to show or to suggest the excellence of either. These poems are coherent and complete as trees or flowers; they cannot be split up and parcelled out like a mosaic of artificial jewellery, which might be taken to pieces by the same artisan who put it together. It must then be remembered that any mere selection from the verse of Byron, however much of care and of good-will be spent upon the task, must perforce either exclude or impair his very greatest work. Cancel or select a leaf from these poems, and you will injure the whole framework equally in either case. It is not without reluctance that I have given any extracts from " Don Juan;" it is not without a full sense of the damage done to these extracts by the very act of extraction. But I could only have left them untouched with a reluctance even greater; and this plea, if it can, must excuse me. As fragments they are exquisite and noble, like the broken hand or severed foot of a Greek statue; but here as much is lost as there. Taken with their context, they regain as much of beauty and of force as the sculptured foot or hand when, reunited to the perfect body, they resume their place and office among its vital and various limbs. This gift of life and variety is the supreme quality of Byron's chief poem; a quality which cannot be expressed by any system of extracts. Little can here be given beyond a sample or two of tragic and serious work. The buoyant beauty of surrounding verse, the " innumerable laughter" and the profound murmur of its many measures, the fervent flow of stanzas now like the ripples and now like the gulfs of the sea, can no more be shown by process of selection than any shallow salt pool left in the sand for sunbeams to drain dry can show the depth and length of the receding tide.

It would be waste of words and time here to en-
large at all upon the excellence of the pure comedy
of " Don Juan." From the first canto to the sixteenth;
from the defence of Julia, which is worthy of Congreve
or Molière, to the study of Adeline, which is worthy
of Laclos or Balzac; the elastic energy of humour
never falters or flags. English criticism, with a
mournful murmur of unanimous virtue, did at the
time, and may yet if it please, appeal against the
satire which strikes home and approve the satire that
flies abroad. It was said, and perhaps is still said,
that the poem falls off and runs low towards the end.
Those who can discover where a change for the worse
begins might at least indicate the landmark, imper-
ceptible to duller eyes, which divides the good from
the bad. Others meantime will retain their belief that
this cry was only raised because in these latter cantos
a certain due amount of satire fell upon the false and
corrupt parts of English character, its mealy-mouthed
vices and its unsound virtues. Had the scene been
shifted to Italy or France, we might have heard little
of the poet's failing power and perverse injustice.

It is just worth a word of notice that Byron, like
Fielding before him, has caught up a well-known name
and prefixed it to his work, without any attempt or
desire to retain the likeness or follow the tradition

attached to it. With him, Don Juan is simply a man somewhat handsomer and luckier than others of his age. This hero is not even a reduced copy of the great and terrible figure with which he has nothing in common but a name. The Titan of embodied evil, the likeness of sin made flesh, which grew up in the grave and bitter imagination of a Spanish poet, steeped in the dyes and heated by the flames of hell, appears even in the hands of Molière diminished, and fallen as it were from Satan to Belial; but still splendid with intellect and courage that tower above the meaner minds and weaker wills of women and of men; still inflexible to human appeal and indomitable by divine anger. To crush him, heaven is compelled to use thunder and hell-fire; and by these, though stricken, he is not subdued. The sombre background of a funereal religion is not yet effaced; but it tasked the whole strength of Molière, gigantic as that strength was, to grapple with the shadow of this giant, to transfigure upon a new stage the tragic and enormous incarnation of supreme sin. As it is, even when playing with his debtors or his peasants, the hero of Molière retains always some feature of his first likeness, some shadow of his early shape. But further than France the terrible legend has never moved. Rigid criticism would therefore say that the title of Byron's masterpiece was properly a misnomer: which is no great matter after all, since the new Juan can never be confounded with the old.

Of Byron's smaller poems there is less to say, and less space to say it. Their splendid merits and their visible defects call neither for praise nor blame. Their place and his, in the literature of England, are fixed points: no critical astronomy of the future can lower or can raise them: they have their own station for all time among the greater and the lesser stars. As a poet, Byron was surpassed, beyond all question and all comparison, by three men at least of his own time; and matched, if not now and then over-matched, by one or two others. The verse of Wordsworth, at its highest, went higher than his; the verse of Landor flowed clearer. But his own ground, where none but he could set foot, was lofty enough, fertile and various. Nothing in Byron is so worthy of wonder and admiration as the scope and range of his power. New fields and ways of work, had he lived, might have given room for exercise and matter for triumph to "that most fiery spirit."* As it is, his work was done

---

* The noble verses of Shelley are fitter to be spoken over Byron than over any first or last Napoleon. To no other man could they be so well applied: for the world indeed took more

at Missolonghi; all of his work for which the fates
could spare him time. A little space was allowed him
to show at least a heroic purpose, and attest a high
design; then, with all things unfinished before him
and behind, he fell asleep after many troubles and
triumphs. Few can ever have gone wearier to the
grave; none with less fear. He had done enough to
earn his rest. Forgetful now and set free for ever
from all faults and foes, he passed through the door-
way of no ignoble death out of reach of time, out of
sight of love, out of hearing of hatred, beyond the
blame of England and the praise of Greece. In the
full strength of spirit and of body his destiny overtook
him, and made an end of all his labours. He had
seen and borne and achieved more than most men
on record. " He was a great man, good at many

of warmth from the fire of his spirit while alive than from any
other then kindled :—

> What! alive and so bold, O Earth!
> Art thou not over-bold?
> What! leapest thou forth as of old
> In the light of thy morning mirth,
> The last of the flock of the starry fold?
> *   *   *   *   *
> Thou wert warming thy fingers old
> O'er the embers covered and cold
> Of that most fiery spirit, when it fled:
> What, Mother, do you laugh now he is dead?

things, and now he has attained this also, to be at rest."

Of the workman and his work there is here no space to say more; and of the present book of selections not much need be said. It bears on the face of it the marks of imperfection and inadequacy; for these the very circumstances and conditions of its existence must be in some part answerable. Adequate and complete such a book cannot be : it must have fallen yet further short of its proper aim, but for the courtesy of those with whom it rested to determine whether the attempt should be made at all. Thanks are therefore due to the publisher and proprietor of Byron's poems, if there should be anything here worth thanks, from the reader; from the editor and publisher of this book, they are due in any case. Much that should be found here will be missed, and by none more than by me; but nothing at least will be found unworthy to share or unfit to secure the fame of Byron.

A. C. SWINBURNE.

CHRISTMAS: 1865.

CONTENTS.

WHEN WE TWO PARTED.

WHEN we two parted
　In silence and tears,
Half broken-hearted
　To sever for years,
Pale grew thy cheek and cold,
　Colder thy kiss;
Truly that hour foretold
　Sorrow to this.

The dew of the morning
　Sunk chill on my brow—
It felt like the warning
　Of what I feel now.
Thy vows are all broken,
　And light is thy fame:
I hear thy name spoken,
　And share in its shame.

B

They name thee before me,
   A knell to mine ear;
A shudder comes o'er me—
   Why wert thou so dear?
They know not I knew thee,
   Who knew thee too well:—
Long, long shall I rue thee,
   Too deeply to tell.

In secret we met—
   In silence I grieve,
That thy heart could forget,
   Thy spirit deceive.
If I should meet thee
   After long years,
How should I greet thee?—
   With silence and tears.

FILL THE GOBLET AGAIN.

A SONG.

FILL the goblet again! for I never before
Felt the glow which now gladdens my heart to its core;
Let us drink!—who would not?—since, through life's
    varied round,
In the goblet alone no deception is found.

I have tried in its turn all that life can supply;
I have bask'd in the beam of a dark rolling eye;
I have loved!—who has not?—but what heart can
    declare
That pleasure existed while passion was there?

In the days of my youth, when the heart's in its
    spring,
And dreams that affection can never take wing,

I had friends!—who has not?—but what tongue will
    avow,
That friends, rosy wine! are so faithful as thou?

The heart of a mistress some boy may estrange,
Friendship shifts with the sunbeam—thou never canst
    change;
Thou grow'st old—who does not?—but on earth what
    appears,
Whose virtues, like thine, still increase with its years?

Yet if blest to the utmost that love can bestow,
Should a rival bow down to our idol below,
We are jealous!—who's not?—thou hast no such alloy;
For the more that enjoy thee, the more we enjoy.

Then the season of youth and its vanities past,
For refuge we fly to the goblet at last;
There we find—do we not?—in the flow of the soul,
That truth, as of yore, is confined to the bowl.

When the box of Pandora was opened on earth,
And Misery's triumph commenced over Mirth,
Hope was left,—was she not?—but the goblet we
    kiss,
And care not for Hope, who are certain of bliss.

Long life to the grape! for when summer is flown,
The age of our nectar shall gladden our own:
We must die—who shall not?—May our sins be for-
given,
And Hebe shall never be idle in heaven.

STANZAS WRITTEN IN PASSING THE AMBRACIAN GULF.

THROUGH cloudless skies, in silvery sheen,
Full beams the moon on Actium's coast:
And on these waves, for Egypt's queen,
The ancient world was won and lost.

And now upon the scene I look,
The azure grave of many a Roman;
Where stern Ambition once forsook
His wavering crown to follow woman.

Florence! whom I will love as well
As ever yet was said or sung
(Since Orpheus sang his spouse from hell),
Whilst thou art fair and I am young;

Sweet Florence! those were pleasant times,
   When worlds were staked for ladies' eyes:
Had bards as many realms as rhymes,
   Thy charms might raise new Antonies.

Though Fate forbids such things to be,
   Yet, by thine eyes and ringlets curl'd!
I cannot lose a world for thee,
   But would not lose thee for a world.

AND THOU ART DEAD, AS YOUNG AND FAIR.

" Heu, quanto minus est cum reliquis versari quam tui meminisse ! "

AND thou art dead, as young and fair
  As aught of mortal birth ;
And form so soft, and charms so rare,
  Too soon return'd to Earth !
Though Earth received them in her bed,
And o'er the spot the crowd may tread
  In carelessness or mirth,
There is an eye which could not brook
A moment on that grave to look.

I will not ask where thou liest low,
  Nor gaze upon the spot ;
There flowers or weeds at will may grow,
  So I behold them not :

It is enough for me to prove
That what I loved, and long must love,
   Like common earth can rot;
To me there needs no stone to tell,
'Tis Nothing that I loved so well.

Yet did I love thee to the last
   As fervently as thou,
Who didst not change through all the past,
   And canst not alter now.
The love where Death has set his seal,
Nor age can chill, nor rival steal,
   Nor falsehood disavow:
And, what were worse, thou canst not see
Or wrong, or change, or fault in me.

The better days of life were ours;
   The worst can be but mine:
The sun that cheers, the storm that lowers,
   Shall never more be thine.
The silence of that dreamless sleep
I envy now too much to weep;
   Nor need I to repine,
That all those charms have pass'd away;
I might have watch'd through long decay.

The flower in ripen'd bloom unmatch'd
    Must fall the earliest prey;
Though by no hand untimely snatch'd,
    The leaves must drop away:
And yet it were a greater grief
To watch it withering, leaf by leaf,
    Than see it pluck'd to-day;
Since earthly eye but ill can bear
To trace the change to foul from fair.

I know not if I could have borne
    To see thy beauties fade;
The night that follow'd such a morn
    Had worn a deeper shade:
Thy day without a cloud hath pass'd,
And thou wert lovely to the last;
    Extinguish'd, not decay'd;
As stars that shoot along the sky
Shine brightest as they fall from high.

As once I wept, if I could weep,
    My tears might well be shed,
To think I was not near to keep
    One vigil o'er thy bed;

To gaze, how fondly! on thy face,
To fold thee in a faint embrace,
   Uphold thy drooping head;
And show that love, however vain,
Nor thou nor I can feel again.

Yet how much less it were to gain,
   Though thou hast left me free,
The loveliest things that still remain,
   Than thus remember thee!
The all of thine that cannot die
Through dark and dread Eternity
   Returns again to me,
And more thy buried love endears
Than aught, except its living years.

From "*CHILDE HAROLD'S PILGRIMAGE.*'

CANTO I.

"ADIEU, adieu! my native shore
    Fades o'er the waters blue;
The night-winds sigh, the breakers roar,
    And shrieks the wild sea-mew.
Yon sun that sets upon the sea
    We follow in his flight;
Farewell awhile to him and thee,
    My native Land—Good Night!

"A few short hours and he will rise
    To give the morrow birth;
And I shall hail the main and skies,
    But not my mother earth.
Deserted is my own good hall,
    Its hearth is desolate;
Wild weeds are gathering on the wall;
    My dog howls at the gate.

" Come hither, hither, my little page !
  Why dost thou weep and wail ?
Or dost thou dread the billows' rage,
  Or tremble at the gale ?
But dash the tear-drop from thine eye ;
  Our ship is swift and strong :
Our fleetest falcon scarce can fly
  More merrily along."

" Let winds be shrill, let waves roll high,
  I fear not wave nor wind :
Yet marvel not, Sir Childe, that I
  Am sorrowful in mind ;
For I have from my father gone,
  A mother whom I love,
And have no friend, save these alone,
  But thee—and one above.

" My father bless'd me fervently,
  Yet did not much complain ;
But sorely will my mother sigh
  Till I come back again."—
" Enough, enough, my little lad !
  Such tears become thine eye ;
If I thy guileless bosom had,
  Mine own would not be dry.

" Come hither, hither, my staunch yeoman,
    Why dost thou look so pale ?
Or dost thou dread a French foeman ?
    Or shiver at the gale ? "—
" Deem'st thou I tremble for my life ?
    Sir Childe, I'm not so weak ;
But thinking on an absent wife
    Will blanch a faithful cheek.

" My spouse and boys dwell near thy hall,
    Along the bordering lake,
And when they on their father call,
    What answer shall she make ? "—
" Enough, enough, my yeoman good,
    Thy·grief let none gainsay ;
But I, who am of lighter mood,
    Will laugh to flee away.

" For who would trust the seeming sighs
    Of wife or paramour ?
Fresh feeres will dry the bright blue eyes
    We late saw streaming o'er.
For pleasures past I do not grieve,
    Nor perils gathering near ;
My greatest grief is that I leave
    No thing that claims a tear.

"And now I'm in the world alone,
    Upon the wide, wide sea:
But why should I for others groan,
    When none will sigh for me?
Perchance my dog will whine in vain,
    Till fed by stranger hands; '
But long ere I come back again
    He'd tear me where he stands.

"With thee, my bark, I'll swiftly go
    Athwart the foaming brine;
Nor care what land thou bear'st me to,
    So not again to mine.
Welcome, welcome, ye dark-blue waves!
    And when you fail my sight,
Welcome, ye deserts and ye caves!
    My native Land—Good Night!"

From CANTO II.

SON of the morning, rise! approach you here!
Come—but molest not yon defenceless urn:
Look on this spot—a nation's sepulchre!
Abode of gods, whose shrines no longer burn.

Even gods must yield—religions take their turn:
'Twas Jove's—'tis Mahomet's—and other creeds
Will rise with other years, till man shall learn
Vainly his incense soars, his victim bleeds;
Poor child of Doubt and Death, whose hope is built
   on reeds.

Bound to the earth, he lifts his eye to heaven—
Is't not enough, unhappy thing! to know
Thou art? Is this a boon so kindly given,
That being, thou wouldst be again, and go,
Thou know'st not, reck'st not, to what region, so
On earth no more, but mingled with the skies?
Still wilt thou dream on future joy and woe?
Regard and weigh yon dust before it flies:
That little urn saith more than thousand homilies.

Or burst the vanish'd Hero's lofty mound;
Far on the solitary shore he sleeps:
He fell, and falling nations mourn'd around;
But now not one of saddening thousands weeps,
Nor warlike worshipper his vigil keeps
Where demi-gods appear'd, as records tell.
Remove yon skull from out the scatter'd heaps:
Is that a temple where a God may dwell?
Why ev'n the worm at last disdains her shatter'd cell!

Look on its broken arch, its ruin'd wall,
Its chambers desolate, and portals foul :
Yes, this was once Ambition's airy hall,
The dome of Thought, the palace of the Soul :
Behold through each lack-lustre, eyeless hole,
The gay recess of Wisdom and of Wit,
And Passion's host, that never brook'd control :
Can all saint, sage, or sophist ever writ,
People this lonely tower, this tenement refit ?

Well didst thou speak, Athena's wisest son !
"All that we know is, nothing can be known."
Why should we shrink from what we cannot shun ?
Each hath his pang, but feeble sufferers groan
With brain-born dreams of evil all their own.
Pursue what Chance or Fate proclaimeth best ;
Peace waits us on the shores of Acheron :
There no forced banquet claims the sated guest,
But Silence spreads the couch of ever welcome rest.

From CANTO III.

AND there they stand, as stands a lofty mind,
Worn, but unstooping to the baser crowd,
All tenantless, save to the crannying wind,
Or holding dark communion with the cloud.

There was a day when they were young and proud;
Banners on high, and battles pass'd below ;
But they who fought are in a bloody shroud,
And those which waved are shredless dust ere now,
And the bleak battlements shall bear no future blow.

Beneath these battlements, within those walls,
Power dwelt amidst her passions ; in proud state
Each robber chief upheld his armed halls,
Doing his evil will, nor less elate
Than mightier heroes of a longer date.
What want these outlaws conquerors should have
But history's purchased page to call them great?
A wider space, an ornamented grave?
Their hopes were not less warm, their souls were full as
    brave.

In their baronial feuds and single fields,
What deeds of prowess unrecorded died !
And Love, which lent a blazon to their shields,
With emblems well devised by amorous pride,
Through all the mail of iron hearts would glide ;
But still their flame was fierceness, and drew on
Keen contest and destruction near allied,
And many a tower for some fair mischief won,
Saw the discolour'd Rhine beneath its ruin run.

c

But Thou, exulting and abounding river !
Making thy waves a blessing as they flow
Through banks whose beauty would endure for ever
Could man but leave thy bright creation so,
Nor its fair promise from the surface mow
With the sharp scythe of conflict,—then to see
Thy valley of sweet waters, were to know
Earth paved like Heaven ; and to seem such to me,
Even now what wants thy stream ?—that it should
    Lethe be.

THE castled crag of Drachenfels
Frowns o'er the wide and winding Rhine,
Whose breast of waters broadly swells
Between the banks which bear the vine,
And hills all rich with blossom'd trees,
And fields which promise corn and wine
And scatter'd cities crowning these,
Whose far white walls along them shine,
Have strew'd a scene, which I should see
With double joy wert *thou* with me.

And peasant girls, with deep blue eyes,
And hands which offer early flowers,

Walk smiling o'er this paradise ;
Above, the frequent feudal towers
Through green leaves lift their walls of gray;
And many a rock which steeply lowers,
And noble arch in proud decay,
Look o'er this vale of vintage-bowers ;
But one thing want these banks of Rhine,—
Thy gentle hand to clasp in mine !

I send the lilies given to me ;
Though long before thy hand they touch,
I know that they must wither'd be,
But yet reject them not as such;
For I have cherish'd them as dear,
Because they yet may meet thine eye,
And guide.thy soul to mine even here,
When thou behold'st them drooping nigh,
And know'st them gather'd by the Rhine,
And offer'd from my heart to thine !

The river nobly foams and flows,
The charm of this enchanted ground,
And all its thousand turns disclose
Some fresher beauty varying round :
The haughtiest breast its wish might bound
Through life to dwell delighted here ;

Nor could on earth a spot be found
To nature and to me so dear,
Could thy dear eyes in following mine
Still sweeten more these banks of Rhine !

THE sky is changed!—and such a change! Oh night,
And storm, and darkness, ye are wondrous strong,
Yet lovely in your strength, as is the light
Of a dark eye in woman ! Far along,
From peak to peak, the rattling crags among
Leaps the live thunder ! Not from one lone cloud,
But every mountain now hath found a tongue,
And Jura answers, through her misty shroud,
Back to the joyous Alps, who call to her aloud !

And this is in the night :—Most glorious night !
Thou wert not sent for slumber ! let me be
A sharer in thy fierce and far delight,—
A portion of the tempest and of thee !
How the lit lake shines, a phosphoric sea,
And the big rain comes dancing to the earth !
And now again 'tis black,—and now, the glee
Of the loud hills shakes with its mountain-mirth,
As if they did rejoice o'er a young earthquake's birth.

Now, where the swift Rhone cleaves his way between
Heights which appear as lovers who have parted
In hate, whose mining depths so intervene,
That they can meet no more, though broken-hearted;
Though in their souls, which thus each other
  thwarted,
Love was the very root of the fond rage
Which blighted their life's bloom, and then departed:
Itself expired, but leaving them an age
Of years all winters,—war within themselves to wage.

Now, where the quick Rhone thus hath cleft his way,
The mightiest of the storms hath ta'en his stand :
For here, not one, but many, make their play,
And fling their thunder-bolts from hand to hand,
Flashing and cast around : of all the band,
The brightest through these parted hills hath fork'd
His lightnings,—as if he did understand,
That in such gaps as desolation work'd,
There the hot shaft should blast whatever therein
  lurk'd.

Sky, mountains, river, winds, lake, lightnings ! ye !
With night, and clouds, and thunder, and a soul
To make these felt and feeling, well may be
Things that have made me watchful ; the far roll

Of your departing voices, is the knoll
Of what in me is sleepless,—if I rest.
But where of ye, O tempests ! is the goal ?
Are ye like those within the human breast ?
Or do ye find, at length, like eagles, some high nest ?

Could I embody and unbosom now
That which is most within me,—could I wreak
My thoughts upon expression, and thus throw
Soul, heart, mind, passions, feelings, strong or weak,
All that I would have sought, and all I seek,
Bear, know, feel, and yet breathe—into *one* word,
And that one word were Lightning, I would speak ;
But as it is, I live and die unheard,
With a most voiceless thought, sheathing it as a sword.

CLARENS ! by heavenly feet thy paths are trod,—
Undying Love's, who here ascends a throne
To which the steps are mountains ; where the god
Is a pervading life and light,—so shown
Not on those summits solely, nor alone
In the still cave and forest ; o'er the flower
His eye is sparkling, and his breath hath blown,
His soft and summer breath, whose tender power
Passes the strength of storms in their most desolate hour.

All things are here of *him;* from the black pines,
Which are his shade on high, and the loud roar
Of torrents, where he listeneth, to the vines
Which slope his green path downward to the shore,
Where the bow'd waters meet him, and adore,
Kissing his feet with murmurs ; and the wood,
The covert of old trees, with trunks all hoar,
But light leaves, young as joy, stands where it stood,
Offering to him, and his, a populous solitude.

A populous solitude of bees and birds,
And fairy-form'd and many-colour'd things,
Who worship him with notes more sweet than words,
And innocently open their glad wings,
Fearless and full of life : the gush of springs,
And fall of lofty fountains, and the bend
Of stirring branches, and the bud which brings
The swiftest thought of beauty, here extend,
Mingling, and made by Love, unto one mighty end.

———————— —

From CANTO IV.

ROLL on, thou deep and dark blue Ocean—roll !
Ten thousand fleets sweep over thee in vain ;
Man marks the earth with ruin—his control
Stops with the shore ; upon the watery plain

The wrecks are all thy deed, nor doth remain
A shadow of man's ravage, save his own,
When, for a moment, like a drop of rain,
He sinks into thy depths with bubbling groan,
Without a grave, unknell'd, uncoffin'd, and unknown.

His steps are not upon thy paths,—thy fields
Are not a spoil for him,—thou dost arise
And shake him from thee; the vile strength he
    wields
For earth's destruction thou dost all despise,
Spurning him from thy bosom to the skies,
And send'st him, shivering in thy playful spray
And howling, to his Gods, where haply lies
His petty hope in some near port or bay,
And dashest him again to earth :—there let him lay.

The armaments which thunderstrike the walls
Of rock-built cities, bidding nations quake,
And monarchs tremble in their capitals,
The oak leviathans, whose huge ribs make
Their clay creator the vain title take
Of lord of thee, and arbiter of war—
These are thy toys, and, as the snowy flake,
They melt into thy yeast of waves, which mar
Alike the Armada's pride or spoils of Trafalgar.

Thy shores are empires, changed in all save thee—
Assyria, Greece, Rome, Carthage, what are they ?
Thy waters wash'd them power while they were
    free,
And many a tyrant since ; their shores obey
The stranger, slave, or savage ; their decay
Has dried up realms to deserts :—not so thou ;—
Unchangeable, save to thy wild waves' play,
Time writes no wrinkle on thine azure brow :
Such as creation's dawn beheld, thou rollest now.

Thou glorious mirror, where the Almighty's form
Glasses itself in tempests ; in all time,—
Calm or convulsed, in breeze, or gale, or storm,
Icing the pole, or in the torrid clime
Dark-heaving—boundless, endless, and sublime,
The image of eternity, the throne
Of the Invisible ; even from out thy slime
The monsters of the deep are made ; each zone
Obeys thee ; thou goest forth, dread, fathomless,
    alone.

And I have loved thee, Ocean ! and my joy
Of youthful sports was on thy breast to be
Borne, like thy bubbles, onward : from a boy
I wanton'd with thy breakers—they to me

Were a delight; and if the freshening sea
Made them a terror—'twas a pleasing fear,
For I was as it were a child of thee,
And trusted to thy billows far and near,
And laid my hand upon thy mane—as I do here.

From " *THE GIAOUR.*"

HE who hath bent him o'er the dead
Ere the first day of death is fled,
The first dark day of nothingness,
The last of danger and distress,
(Before Decay's effacing fingers
Have swept the lines where beauty lingers,)
And mark'd the mild angelic air,
The rapture of repose that's there,
The fix'd yet tender traits that streak
The languor of the placid cheek,
And—but for that sad shrouded eye,
   That fires not, wins not, weeps not, now,
   And but for that chill, changeless brow,
Where cold Obstruction's apathy
Appals the gazing mourner's heart,
As if to him it could impart

The doom he dreads, yet dwells upon ;
Yes, but for these and these alone,
Some moments, ay, one treacherous hour,
He still might doubt the tyrant's power ;
So fair, so calm, so softly seal'd,
The first, last look by death reveal'd !

SONNET ON CHILLON.

ETERNAL Spirit of the chainless Mind !
  Brightest in dungeons, Liberty ! thou art,
  For there thy habitation is the heart—
The heart which love of thee alone can bind ;
And when thy sons to fetters are consign'd—
  To fetters, and the damp vault's dayless gloom,
  Their country conquers with their martyrdom,
And Freedom's fame finds wings on every wind.
Chillon ! thy prison is a holy place,
  And thy sad floor an altar—for 'twas trod,
Until his very steps have left a trace
  Worn, as if thy cold pavement were a sod,
By Bonnivard ! May none those marks efface !
  For they appeal from tyranny to God.

THE PRISONER OF CHILLON.

My hair is grey, but not with years,
    Nor grew it white
    In a single night,
As men's have grown from sudden fears :
My limbs are bow'd, though not with toil,
    But rusted with a vile repose,
For they have been a dungeon's spoil,
    And mine has been the fate of those
To whom the goodly earth and air
Are bann'd, and barr'd—forbidden fare ;
But this was for my father's faith
I suffer'd chains and courted death ;
That father perish'd at the stake
For tenets he would not forsake ;
And for the same his lineal race
In darkness found a dwelling-place ;

We were seven—who now are one,
  Six in youth, and one in age,
Finish'd as they had begun,
  Proud of Persecution's rage;
One in fire, and two in field,
Their belief with blood have seal'd,
Dying as their father died,
For the God their foes denied;
Three were in a dungeon cast,
Of whom this wreck is left the last.

There are seven pillars of Gothic mould,
In Chillon's dungeons deep and old,
There are seven columns, massy and grey,
Dim with a dull imprison'd ray,
A sunbeam which hath lost its way,
And through the crevice and the cleft
Of the thick wall is fallen and left;
Creeping o'er the floor so damp,
Like a marsh's meteor lamp:
And in each pillar there is a ring,
  And in each ring there is a chain;
That iron is a cankering thing,
  For in these limbs its teeth remain,
With marks that will not wear away,
Till I have done with this new day,

Which now is painful to these eyes,
Which have not seen the sun so rise
For years—I cannot count them o'er,
I lost their long and heavy score,
When my last brother droop'd and died,
And I lay living by his side.

They chain'd us each to a column stone,
And we were three—yet, each alone;
We could not move a single pace,
We could not see each other's face,
But with that pale and livid light
That made us strangers in our sight:
And thus together—yet apart,
Fetter'd in hand, but join'd in heart,
'Twas still some solace, in the dearth
Of the pure elements of earth,
To hearken to each other's speech,
And each turn comforter to each
With some new hope, or legend old,
Or song heroically bold;
But even these at length grew cold.
Our voices took a dreary tone,
An echo of the dungeon stone,
    A grating sound, not full and free,
    As they of yore were wont to be:

It might be fancy, but to me
They never sounded like our own.

I was the eldest of the three,
  And to uphold and cheer the rest
  I ought to do—and did my best—
And each did well in his degree.
  The youngest, whom my father loved,
Because our mother's brow was given
To him, with eyes as blue as heaven—
  For him my soul was sorely moved;
And truly might it be distress'd
To see such bird in such a nest;
For he was beautiful as day—   .
  (When day was beautiful to me
  As to young eagles, being free)—
  A polar day, which will not see
A sunset till its summer's gone,
  Its sleepless summer of long light,
The snow-clad offspring of the sun:
  And thus he was as pure and bright,
And in his natural spirit gay,
With tears for nought but others' ills,
And then they flow'd like mountain rills,
Unless he could assuage the woe
Which he abhorr'd to view below.

The other was as pure of mind,
But form'd to combat with his kind;
Strong in his frame, and of a mood
Which 'gainst the world in war had stood,
And perish'd in the foremost rank
    With joy :—but not in chains to pine :
His spirit wither'd with their clank,
    I saw it silently decline—
And so perchance in sooth did mine :
But yet I forced it on to cheer
Those relics of a home so dear.
He was a hunter of the hills,
    Had follow'd there the deer and wolf;
    To him this dungeon was a gulf,
And fetter'd feet the worst of ills.

Lake Leman lies by Chillon's walls :
A thousand feet in depth below
Its massy waters meet and flow;
Thus much the fathom-line was sent
From Chillon's snow-white battlement,
    Which round about the wave inthralls :
A double dungeon wall and wave
Have made—and like a living grave.
Below the surface of the lake
The dark vault lies wherein we lay,

We heard it ripple night and day ;
  Sounding o'er our heads it knock'd ;
And I have felt the winter's spray
Wash through the bars when winds were high
And wanton in the happy sky ;
  And then the very rock hath rock'd,
  And I have felt it shake, unshock'd,
Because I could have smiled to see
The death that would have set me free.

I said my nearer brother pined,
I said his mighty heart declined,
He loathed and put away his food ;
It was not that 'twas coarse and rude,
For we were used to hunter's fare,
And for the like had little care :
The milk drawn from the mountain goat
Was changed for water from the moat,
Our bread was such as captives' tears
Have moisten'd many a thousand years,
Since man first pent his fellow men
Like brutes within an iron den ;
But what were these to us or him ?
These wasted not his heart or limb ;
My brother's soul was of that mould
Which in a palace had grown cold,

D

Had his free breathing been denied
The range of the steep mountain's side;
But why delay the truth ?—he died.
, I saw, and could not hold his head,
Nor reach his dying hand—nor dead,—
Though hard I strove, but strove in vain,
To rend and gnash my bonds in twain.
He died, and they unlock'd his chain,
And scoop'd for him a shallow grave
Even from the cold earth of our cave.
I begg'd them as a boon to lay
His corse in dust whereon the day
Might shine—it was a foolish thought,
But then within my brain it wrought,
That even in death his freeborn breast
In such a dungeon could not rest.
I might have spared my idle prayer—
They coldly laugh'd, and laid him there :
The flat and turfless earth above
The being we so much did love;
His empty chain above it leant,
Such murder's fitting monument !

But he, the favourite and the flower,
Most cherish'd since his natal hour,
His mother's image in fair face,

The infant love of all his race,
His martyr'd father's dearest thought,
My latest care, for whom I sought
To hoard my life, that his might be
Less wretched now, and one day free ;
He, too, who yet had held untired
A spirit natural or inspired—
He, too, was struck, and day by day
Was wither'd on the stalk away.
Oh, God ! it is a fearful thing
To see the human soul take wing
In any shape, in any mood :
I've seen it rushing forth in blood,
I've seen it on the breaking ocean
Strive with a swoln convulsive motion,
I've seen the sick and ghastly bed
Of Sin delirious with its dread ;
But these were horrors—this was woe
Unmix'd with such—butsure and slow :
He faded, and so calm and meek,
So softly worn, so sweetly weak,
So tearless, yet so tender, kind,
And grieved for those he left behind ;
With all the while a cheek whose bloom
Was as a mockery of the tomb,
Whose tints as gently sunk away

As a departing rainbow's ray ;
An eye of most transparent light,
That almost made the dungeon bright,
And not a word of murmur, not
A groan o'er his untimely lot,—
A little talk of better days,
A little hope my own to raise,
For I was sunk in silence—lost
In this last loss, of all the most ;
And then the sighs he would suppress
Of fainting nature's feebleness,
More slowly drawn, grew less and less :
I listen'd, but I could not hear ;
I call'd, for I was wild with fear ;
I knew 'twas hopeless, but my dread
Would not be thus admonished ;
I call'd, and thought I heard a sound—
I burst my chain with one strong bound,
And rush'd to him :—I found him not,
_I_ only stirr'd in this black spot,
_I_ only lived, _I_ only drew
The accursed breath of dungeon-dew ;
The last, the sole, the dearest link
Between me and the eternal brink,
Which bound me to my failing race,
Was broken in this fatal place.

One on the earth, and one beneath—
My brothers—both had ceased to breathe :
I took that hand which lay so still,
Alas ! my own was full as chill ;
I had not strength to stir, or strive,
But felt that I was still alive—
A frantic feeling, when we know
That what we love shall ne'er be so.
    I know not why
    I could not die,
I had no earthly hope but faith,
And that forbade a selfish death.

What next befell me then and there
    I know not well—I never knew—
First came the' loss of light, and air,
    And then of darkness too :
I had no thought, no feeling—none—
Among the stones I stood a stone,
And was, scarce conscious what I wist,
As shrubless crags within the mist;
For all was blank, and bleak, and grey;
It was not night, it was not day ;
It was not even the dungeon-light,
So hateful to my heavy sight,
But vacancy absorbing space,

And fixedness without a place ;
There were no stars, no earth, no time,
No check, no change, no good, no crime,
But silence, and a stirless breath
Which neither was of life nor death ;
A sea of stagnant idleness,
Blind, boundless, mute, and motionless !

A light broke in upon my brain,—
    It was the carol of a bird ;
It ceased, and then it came again,
    The sweetest song ear ever heard,
And mine was thankful till my eyes
Ran over with the glad surprise,
And they that moment could not see
I was the mate of misery ;
But then by dull degrees came back
My senses to their wonted track ;
I saw the dungeon walls and floor
Close slowly round me as before,
I saw the glimmer of the sun
Creeping as it before had done,
But through the crevice where it came
That bird was perch'd, as fond and tame,
    And tamer than upon the tree ;
A lovely bird, with azure wings,

And song that said a thousand things,
  And seem'd to say them all for me !
I never saw its like before,
I ne'er shall see its likeness more :
It seem'd like me to want a mate,
But was not half so desolate,
And it was come to love me when
None lived to love me so again,
And cheering from my dungeon's brink,
Had brought me back to feel and think.
I know not if it late were free,
  Or broke its cage to perch on mine,
But knowing well captivity,
  Sweet bird ! I could not wish for thine !
Or if it were, in winged guise,
A visitant from Paradise ;
For—Heaven forgive that thought ! the while
Which made me both to weep and smile—
I sometimes deem'd that it might be
My brother's soul come down to me ;
But then at last away it flew,
And then 'twas mortal well I knew,
For he would never thus have flown,
And left me twice so doubly lone,
Lone as the corse within its shroud,
Lone as a solitary cloud,—

A single cloud on a sunny day,
While all the rest of heaven is clear,
A frown upon the atmosphere,
That hath no business to appear
   When skies are blue, and earth is gay.

A kind of change came in my fate,
My keepers grew compassionate;
I know not what had made them so,
They were inured to sights of woe,
But so it was:—my broken chain
With links unfasten'd did remain,
And it was liberty to stride
Along my cell from side to side,
And up and down, and then athwart,
And tread it over every part;
And round the pillars one by one,
Returning where my walk begun,
Avoiding only, as I trod,
My brothers' graves without a sod;
For if I thought with heedless tread
My step profaned their lowly bed,
My breath came gaspingly and thick,
And my crush'd heart fell blind and sick.

I made a footing in the wall,

It was not therefrom to escape,
For I had buried one and all
  Who loved me in a human shape;
And the whole earth would henceforth be
A wider prison unto me:
No child, no sire, no kin had I,
No partner in my misery;
I thought of this, and I was glad,
For thought of them had made me mad;
But I was curious to ascend
To my barr'd windows, and to bend
Once more, upon the mountains high,
The quiet of a loving eye.

I saw them, and they were the same,
They were not changed like me in frame;
I saw there thousand years of snow
On high—their wide long lake below,
And the blue Rhone in fullest flow;
I heard the torrents leap and gush
O'er channell'd rock and broken bush;
I saw the white-wall'd distant town,
And whiter sails go skimming down;
And then there was a little isle,
Which in my very face did smile,
    The only one in view;

A small green isle, it seem'd no more,
Scarce broader than my dungeon floor,
But in it there were three tall trees,
And o'er it blew the mountain breeze,
And by it there were waters flowing,
And on it there were young flowers growing,
    Of gentle breath and hue.
The fish swam by the castle wall,
And they seem'd joyous each and all;
The eagle rode the rising blast,
Methought he never flew so fast
As then to me he seem'd to fly;
And then new tears came in my eye,
And I felt troubled—and would fain
I had not left my recent chain;
And when I did descend again,
The darkness of my dim abode
Fell on me as a heavy load;
It was as is a new-dug grave,
Closing o'er one we sought to save,—
And yet my glance, too much opprest,
Had almost need of such a rest.

It might be months, or years, or days,
    I kept no count, I took no note,
I had no hope my eyes to raise,

And clear them of their dreary mote ;
At last men came to set me free ;
   I ask'd not why, and reck'd not where ;
· It was at length the same to me,
Fetter'd or fetterless to be,
   I learn'd to love despair.
And thus when they appear'd at last,
And all my bonds aside were cast,
These heavy walls to me had grown
A hermitage—and all my own !
And half I felt as they were come
To tear me from a second home :
With spiders I had friendship made,
And watch'd them in their sullen trade,
Had seen the mice by moonlight play,
And why should I feel less than they ?
We were all inmates of one place,
And I, the monarch of each race,
Had power to kill—yet, strange to tell !
In quiet we had learn'd to dwell ;
My very chains and I grew friends,
So much a long communion tends
To make us what we are :—even I
Regain'd my freedom with a sigh.

STANZAS TO AUGUSTA.

THOUGH the day of my destiny's over,
  And the star of my fate hath declined,
Thy soft heart refused to discover
  The faults which so many could find ;
Though thy soul with my grief was acquainted,
  It shrunk not to share it with me,
And the love which my spirit hath painted
  It never hath found but in *thee*.

Then when nature around me is smiling,
  The last smile which answers to mine,
I do not believe it beguiling,
  Because it reminds me of thine ;
And when winds are at war with the ocean,
  As the breasts I believed in with me,
If their billows excite an emotion,
  It is that they bear me from *thee*.

Though the rock of my last hope is shiver'd,
And its fragments are sunk in the wave,
Though I feel that my soul is deliver'd
To pain—it shall not be its slave.
There is many a pang to pursue me :
They may crush, but they shall not contemn ;
They may torture, but shall not subdue me ;
'Tis of *thee* that I think—not of them.

Though human, thou didst not deceive me,
Though woman, thou didst not forsake,
Though loved, thou forborest to grieve me,
Though slander'd, thou never couldst shake ;
Though trusted, thou didst not disclaim me,
Though parted, it was not to fly,
Though watchful, 'twas not to defame me,
Nor, mute, that the world might belie.

Yet I blame not the world, nor despise it,
Nor the war of the many with one ;
If my soul was not fitted to prize it,
'Twas folly not sooner to shun :
And if dearly that error hath cost me,
And more than I once could foresee,
I have found that, whatever it lost me,
It could not deprive me of *thee.*

From the wreck of the past, which hath perish'd,
　　Thus much I at least may recall,
It hath taught me that what I most cherish'd
　　Deserved to be dearest of all:
In the desert a fountain is springing,
　　In the wide waste there still is a tree,
And a bird in the solitude singing,
　　Which speaks to my spirit of *thee*.

EPISTLE TO AUGUSTA.

My sister! my sweet sister! if a name
Dearer and purer were, it should be thine ;
Mountains and seas divide us, but I claim
No tears, but tenderness to answer mine :
Go where I will, to me thou art the same—
A loved regret which I would not resign.
There yet are two things in my destiny,—
A world to roam through, and a home with thee.

The first were nothing—had I still the last,
It were the haven of my happiness ;
But other claims and other ties thou hast,
And mine is not the wish to make them less.
A strange doom is thy father's son's, and past
Recalling, as it lies beyond redress ;
Reversed for him our grandsire's fate of yore,—
He had no rest at sea, nor I on shore.

If my inheritance of storms hath been
In other elements, and on the rocks
Of perils, overlook'd or unforeseen,
I have sustain'd my share of worldly shocks,
The fault was mine ; nor do I seek to screen
My errors with defensive paradox ;
I have been cunning in mine overthrow,
The careful pilot of my proper woe.

Mine were my faults, and mine be their reward.
My whole life was a contest, since the day
That gave me being, gave me that which marr'd
The gift,—a fate, or will, that walk'd astray ;
And I at times have found the struggle hard,
And thought of shaking off my bonds of clay :
But now I fain would for a time survive,
If but to see what next can well arrive.

Kingdoms and empires in my little day
I have outlived, and yet I am not old ;
And when I look on this, the petty spray
Of my own years of trouble, which have roll'd
Like a wild bay of breakers, melts away :
Something—I know not what—does still uphold
A spirit of slight patience ;—not in vain, .
Even for its own sake, do we purchase pain.

Perhaps the workings of defiance stir
Within me—or perhaps a cold despair,
Brought on when ills habitually recur,—
Perhaps a kinder clime, or purer air,
(For even to this may change of soul refer,
And with light armour we may learn to bear,)
Have taught me a strange quiet, which was not
The chief companion of a calmer lot.

I feel almost at times as I have felt
In happy childhood; trees, and flowers, and brooks,
Which do remember me of where I dwelt
Ere my young mind was sacrificed to books,
Come as of yore upon me, and can melt
My heart with recognition of their looks ;
And even at moments I could think I see
Some living thing to love—but none like thee.

Here are the Alpine landscapes which create
A fund for contemplation ; to admire
Is a brief feeling of a trivial date ;
But something worthier do such scenes inspire :
Here to be lonely is not desolate,
For much I view which I could most desire,
And, above all, a lake I can behold
Lovelier, not dearer, than our own of old.

E

Oh that thou wert but with me !—but I grow
The fool of my own wishes, and forget
The solitude which I have vaunted so
Has lost its praise in this but one regret ;
There may be others which I less may show ;—
I am not of the plaintive mood, and yet
I feel an ebb in my philosophy,
And the tide rising in my alter'd eye.

I did remind thee of our own dear Lake,
By the old Hall which may be mine no more.
Leman's is fair ; but think not I forsake
The sweet remembrance of a dearer shore :
Sad havoc Time must with my memory make,
Ere *that* or *thou* can fade these eyes before ;
Though, like all things which I have loved, they are
Resign'd for ever, or divided far.

The world is all before me ; I but ask
Of Nature that with which she will comply—
It is but in her summer's sun to bask,
To mingle with the quiet of her sky,
To see her gentle face without a mask,
And never gaze on it with apathy.
She was my early friend, and now shall be
My sister—till I look again on thee.

I can reduce all feelings but this one ;
And that I would not ;—for at length I see
Such scenes as those wherein my life begun.
The earliest—even the only paths for me—
Had I but sooner learnt the crowd to shun,
I had been better than I now can be ;
The passions which have torn me would have slept;
I had not suffer'd, and *thou* hadst not wept.

With false Ambition what had I to do ?
Little with Love, and least of all with Fame ;
And yet they came unsought, and with me grew,
And made me all which they can make—a name.
Yet this was not the end I did pursue ;
Surely I once beheld a nobler aim.
But all is over—I am one the more
To baffled millions which have gone before.

And for the future, this world's future may
From me demand but little of my care ;
I have outlived myself by many a day ;
Having survived so many things that were ;
My years have been no slumber, but the prey
Of ceaseless vigils ; for I had the share
Of life which might have fill'd a century,
Before its fourth in time had pass'd me by.

And for the remnant which may be to come
I am content ; and for the past I feel
Not thankless,—for within the crowded sum
Of struggles, happiness at times would steal,
And for the present, I would not benumb
My feelings further.—Nor shall I conceal
That with all this I still can look around,
And worship Nature with a thought profound.

For thee, my own sweet sister, in thy heart
I know myself secure, as thou in mine ;
We were and are—I am, even as thou art—
Beings who ne'er each other can resign ;
It is the same, together or apart,
From life's commencement to its slow decline
We are entwined—let death come slow or fast,
The tie which bound the first endures the last !

THE DREAM.

OUR life is two-fold: Sleep hath its own world,
A boundary between the things misnamed
Death and existence: Sleep hath its own world,
And a wide realm of wild reality.
And dreams in their development have breath,
And tears, and tortures, and the touch of joy;
They leave a weight upon our waking thoughts,
They take a weight from off our waking toils,
They do divide our being; they become
A portion of ourselves as of our time,
And look like heralds of eternity;
They pass like spirits of the past,—they speak
Like Sibyls of the future: they have power—
The tyranny of pleasure and of pain;
They make us what we were not—what they will,
And shake us with the vision that's gone by,
The dread of vanish'd shadows—Are they so?

Is not the past all shadow?—What are they?
Creations of the mind?—The mind can make
Substance, and people planets of its own
With beings brighter than have been, and give
A breath to forms which can outlive all flesh.
I would recall a vision which I dream'd
Perchance in sleep—for in itself a thought,
A slumbering thought, is capable of years,
And curdles a long life into one hour.

I saw two beings in the hues of youth
Standing upon a hill, a gentle hill,
Green and of mild declivity, the last
As 'twere the cape of a long ridge of such,
Save that there was no sea to lave its base,
But a most living landscape, and the wave
Of woods and corn-fields, and the abodes of men
Scatter'd at intervals, and wreathing smoke
Arising from such rustic roofs ;—the hill
Was crown'd with a peculiar diadem
Of trees, in circular array, so fix'd,
Not by the sport of nature; but of man :
These two, a maiden and a youth, were there
Gazing—the one on all that was beneath
Fair as herself—but the boy gazed on her ;
And both were young, and one was beautiful :

And both were young—yet not alike in youth.
As the sweet moon on the horizon's verge,
The maid was on the eve of womanhood ;
The boy had fewer summers, but his heart
Had far outgrown his years, and to his eye
There was but one beloved face on earth,
And that was shining on him : he had look'd
Upon it till it could not pass away ;
He had no breath, no being, but in hers ;
She was his voice ; he did not speak to her,
But trembled on her words ; she was his sight,
For his eye follow'd hers, and saw with hers,
Which colour'd all his objects :—he had ceased
To live within himself ; she was his life,
The ocean to the river of his thoughts,
Which terminated all : upon a tone,
A touch of hers, his blood would ebb and flow,
And his cheek change tempestuously—his heart
Unknowing of its cause of agony.
But she in these fond feelings had no share :
Her sighs were not for him ; to her he was
Even as a brother—but no more ; 'twas much,
For brotherless she was, save in the name
Her infant friendship had bestow'd on him ;
Herself the solitary scion left
Of a time-honour'd race.—It was a name

Which pleased him, and yet pleased him not—and why?
Time taught him a deep answer—when she loved
Another; even *now* she loved another,
And on the summit of that hill she stood
Looking afar if yet her lover's steed
Kept pace with her expectancy, and flew.

A change came o'er the spirit of my dream.
There was an ancient mansion, and before
Its walls there was a steed caparison'd:
Within an antique Oratory stood
The Boy of whom I spake;—he was alone,
And pale, and pacing to and fro: anon
He sate him down, and seized a pen, and traced
Words which I could not guess of; then he lean'd
His bow'd head on his hands, and shook as 'twere
With a convulsion—then rose again,
And with his teeth and quivering hands did tear
What he had written, but he shed no tears,
And he did calm himself, and fix his brow
Into a kind of quiet: as he paused,
The Lady of his love re-entered there;
She was serene and smiling then, and yet
She knew she was by him beloved,—she knew,
For quickly comes such knowledge, that his heart
Was darken'd with her shadow, and she saw

That he was wretched, but she saw not all.
He rose, and with a cold and gentle grasp
He took her hand; a moment o'er his face
A tablet of unutterable thoughts
Was traced, and then it faded, as it came;
He dropp'd the hand he held, and with slow steps
Retired, but not as bidding her adieu,
For they did part with mutual smiles; he pass'd
From out the massy gate of that old Hall,
And mounting on his steed he went his way;
And ne'er repass'd that hoary threshold more.

A change came o'er the spirit of my dream.
The Boy was sprung to manhood: in the wilds
Of fiery climes he made himself a home,
And his soul drank their sunbeams: he was girt
With strange and dusky aspects; he was not
Himself like what he had been; on the sea
And on the shore he was a wanderer;
There was a mass of many images
Crowded like waves upon me, but he was
A part of all; and in the last he lay
Reposing from the noontide sultriness,
Couch'd among fallen columns, in the shade
Of ruin'd walls that had survived the names
Of those who rear'd them; by his sleeping side

Stood camels grazing, and some goodly steeds
Were fasten'd near a fountain ; and a man
Clad in a flowing garb did watch the while,
While many of his tribe slumber'd around :
And they were canopied by the blue sky,
So cloudless, clear, and purely beautiful,
That God alone was to be seen in heaven.

A change came o'er the spirit of my dream.
The Lady of his love was wed with One
Who did not love her better :—in her home,
A thousand leagues from his,—her native home,
She dwelt, begirt with growing Infancy,
Daughters and sons of Beauty,—but behold !
Upon her face there was the tint of grief,
The settled shadow of an inward strife,
And an unquiet drooping of the eye,
As if its lid were charged with unshed tears.
What could her grief be ?—she had all she loved,
And he who had so loved her was not there
To trouble with bad hopes, or evil wish,
Or ill-repress'd affliction, her pure thoughts.
What could her grief be ?—she had loved him not,
Nor given him cause to deem himself beloved,
Nor could he be a part of that which prey'd
Upon her mind—a spectre of the past.

A change came o'er the spirit of my dream.
The Wanderer was return'd.—I saw him stand
Before an Altar—with a gentle bride;
Her face was fair, but was not that which made
The Starlight of his Boyhood;—as he stood
Even at the altar, o'er his brow there came
The self-same aspect, and the quivering shock
That in the antique Oratory shook
His bosom in its solitude; and then—
As in that hour—a moment o'er his face
The tablet of unutterable thoughts
Was traced,—and then it faded as it came,
And he stood calm and quiet, and he spoke
The fitting vows, but heard not his own words,
And all things reel'd around him; he could see
Not that which was, nor that which should have been—
But the old mansion, and the accustom'd hall,
And the remember'd chambers, and the place,
The day, the hour, the sunshine, and the shade,
All things pertaining to that place and hour,
And her who was his destiny,—came back
And thrust themselves between him and the light:
What business had they there at such a time?

A change came o'er the spirit of my dream.
The Lady of his love;—Oh! she was changed

As by the sickness of the soul ; her mind
Had wander'd from its dwelling, and her eyes
They had not their own lustre, but the look
Which is not of the earth ; she was become
The queen of a fantastic realm ; her thoughts
Were combinations of disjointed things ;
And forms impalpable and unperceived
Of others' sight familiar were to hers.
And this the world calls frenzy ; but the wise
Have a far deeper madness, and the glance
Of melancholy is a fearful gift ;
What is it but the telescope of truth ?
Which strips the distance of its fantasies,
And brings life near in utter nakedness,
Making the cold reality too real !

A change came o'er the spirit of my dream.
The Wanderer was alone as heretofore,
The beings which surrounded him were gone,
Or were at war with him ; he was a mark
For blight and desolation, compass'd round
With Hatred and Contention ; Pain was mix'd
In all which was served up to him, until,
Like to the Pontic monarch of old days,
He fed on poisons, and they had no power,
But were a kind of nutriment ; he lived

Through that which had been death to many men,
And made him friends of mountains: with the stars
And the quick Spirit of the Universe
He held his dialogues; and they did teach
To him the magic of their mysteries;
To him the book of Night was open'd wide,
And voices from the deep abyss reveal'd
A marvel and a secret—Be it so.

My dream was past; it had no further change.
It was of a strange order, that the doom
Of these two creatures should be thus traced out
Almost like a reality—the one
To end in madness—both in misery.

PROMETHEUS.

TITAN! to whose immortal eyes
　The sufferings of mortality,
　Seen in their sad reality,
Were not as things that gods despise;
What was thy pity's recompense?
A silent suffering, and intense;
The rock, the vulture, and the chain,
All that the proud can feel of pain,
The agony they do not show,
The suffocating sense of woe,
　Which speaks but in its loneliness,
And then is jealous lest the sky
Should have a listener, nor will sigh
　Until its voice is echoless.

Titan! to thee the strife was given
　Between the suffering and the will,

Which torture where they cannot kill;
And the inexorable Heaven,
And the deaf tyranny of Fate,
The ruling principle of Hate,
Which for its pleasure doth create
The things it may annihilate,
Refused thee even the boon to die:
The wretched gift eternity
Was thine—and thou hast borne it well.
All that the Thunderer wrung from thee
Was but the menace which flung back
On him the torments of thy rack;
The fate thou didst so well foresee,
But would not to appease him tell;
And in thy Silence was his Sentence,
And in his Soul a vain repentance,
And evil dread so ill dissembled,
That in his hand the lightnings trembled.

Thy Godlike crime was to be kind,
  To render with thy precepts less
  The sum of human wretchedness,
And strengthen Man with his own mind;
But baffled as thou wert from high,
Still in thy patient energy,
In the endurance, and repulse

Of thine impenetrable Spirit,
Which Earth and Heaven could not convulse,
　A mighty lesson we inherit:
Thou art a symbol and a sign
　To Mortals of their fate and force;
Like thee, Man is in part divine,
　A troubled stream from a pure source;
And Man in portions can foresee
His own funereal destiny;
His wretchedness, and his resistance,
And his sad unallied existence:
To which his Spirit may oppose
Itself—and equal to all woes,
　And a firm will, and a deep sense,
Which even in torture can descry
　Its own concenter'd recompense,
Triumphant where it dares defy,
And making Death a Victory.

A FRAGMENT.

WHAT is this Death?—a quiet of the heart?
The whole of that of which we are a part?
For life is but a vision—what I see
Of all which lives alone is life to me,
And being so—the absent are the dead,
Who haunt us from tranquillity, and spread
A dreary shroud around us, and invest
With sad remembrances our hours of rest.
  The absent are the dead—for they are cold,
And ne'er can be what once we did behold;
And they are changed, and cheerless,—or if yet
The unforgotten do not all forget,
Since thus divided—equal must it be
If the deep barrier be of earth, or sea;
It may be both—but one day end it must
In the dark union of insensate dust.

F

The under-earth inhabitants—are they
But mingled millions·decomposed to clay?
The ashes of a thousand ages spread
Wherever man has trodden or shall tread?
Or do they in their silent cities dwell
Each in his incommunicative cell?
Or have they their own language? and a sense
Of breathless being?—darken'd and intense
As midnight in her solitude?—Oh Earth!
Where are the past?—and wherefore had they birth?
The dead are thy inheritors—and we
But bubbles on thy surface; and the key
Of thy profundity is in the grave,
The ebon portal of thy peopled cave,
Where I would walk in spirit, and behold
Our elements resolved to things untold,
And fathom hidden wonders, and explore
The essence of great bosoms now no more.

From "MANFRED."

(A voice is heard in the Incantation which follows.)

When the moon is on the wave,
    And the glow-worm in the grass,
And the meteor on the grave,
    And the wisp on the morass ;
When the falling stars are shooting,
And the answer'd owls are hooting,
And the silent leaves are still
In the shadow of the hill,
Shall my soul be upon thine,
With a power and with a sign.

Though thy slumber may be deep,
Yet thy spirit shall not sleep ;
There are shades which will not vanish,
There are thoughts thou canst not banish ;

F 2

By a power to thee unknown,
Thou canst never be alone ;
Thou art wrapt as with a shroud,
Thou art gather'd in a cloud ;
And for ever shalt thou dwell
In the spirit of this spell.

Though thou seest me not pass by,
Thou shalt feel me with thine eye
As a thing that, though unseen,
Must be near thee, and hath been ;
And when in that secret dread
Thou hast turn'd around thy head,
Thou shalt marvel I am not
As thy shadow on the spot,
And the power which thou dost feel
Shall be what thou must conceal.

And a magic voice and verse
Hath baptized thee with a curse ;
And a spirit of the air
Hath begirt thee with a snare ;
In the wind there is a voice
Shall forbid thee to rejoice ;
And to thee shall night deny
All the quiet of her sky ;

And the day shall have a sun,
Which shall make thee wish it done.

From thy false tears I did distil
An essence which hath strength to kill ;
From thy own heart I then did wring
The black blood in its blackest spring ;
From thy own smile I snatch'd the snake,
For there it coil'd as in a brake ;
From thy own lip I drew the charm
Which gave all these their chiefest harm ;
In proving every poison known,
I found the strongest was thine own.

By thy cold breast and serpent smile,
By thy unfathom'd gulfs of guile,
By that most seeming virtuous eye,
By thy shut soul's hypocrisy ;
By the perfection of thine art
Which pass'd for human thine own heart ;
By thy delight in others' pain,
And by thy brotherhood of Cain,
I call upon thee ! and compel
Thyself to be thy proper Hell !

And on thy head I pour the vial

Which doth devote thee to this trial;
Nor to slumber, nor to die,
Shall be in thy destiny;
Though thy death shall still seem near
To thy wish, but as a fear;
Lo! the spell now works around thee,
And the clankless chain hath bound thee;
O'er thy heart and brain together
Hath the word been pass'd—now wither!

From THE SAME.

The Mountain of the Jungfrau.—Time, Morning.—
MANFRED *alone upon the Cliffs.*

Manfred. THE spirits I have raised abandon me,
The spells which I have studied baffle me,
The remedy I reck'd of tortured me;
I lean no more on superhuman aid;
It hath no power upon the past, and for
The future, till the past be gulf'd in darkness,
It is not of my search.—My mother Earth!
And thou fresh breaking Day, and you, ye Mountains,
Why are ye beautiful? I cannot love ye.
And thou, the bright eye of the universe,
That openest over all, and unto all

Art a delight—thou shin'st not on my heart.
And you, ye crags, upon whose extreme edge
I stand, and on the torrent's brink beneath
Behold the tall pines dwindled as to shrubs
In dizziness of distance; when a leap,
A stir, a motion, even a breath, would bring
My breast upon its rocky bosom's bed
To rest for ever—wherefore do I pause?
I feel the impulse—yet I do not plunge;
I see the peril—yet do not recede;
And my brain reels—and yet my foot is firm:
There is a power upon me which withholds,
And makes it my fatality to live,—
If it be life to wear within myself
This barrenness of spirit, and to be
My own soul's sepulchre, for I have ceased
To justify my deeds unto myself—
The last infirmity of evil.   Ay,
Thou winged and cloud-cleaving minister,

                                        [*An eagle passes.*

Whose happy flight is highest into heaven,
Well may'st thou swoop so near me—I should be
Thy prey, and gorge thine eaglets; thou art gone
Where the eye cannot follow thee; but thine
Yet pierces downward, onward, or above,
With a pervading vision.—Beautiful!

How beautiful is all this visible world!
How glorious in its action and itself!
But we, who name ourselves its sovereigns, we,
Half dust, half deity, alike unfit
To sink or soar, with our mix'd essence make
A conflict of its elements, and breathe
The breath of degradation and of pride,
Contending with low wants and lofty will,
Till our mortality predominates,
And men are—what they name not to themselves,
And trust not to each other.   Hark ! the note,
                    [*The Shepherd's pipe in the distance is heard.*
The natural music of the mountain reed—
For here the patriarchal days are not
A pastoral fable—pipes in the liberal air,
Mix'd with the sweet bells of the sauntering herd ;
My soul would drink those echoes.   Oh, that I were
The viewless spirit of a lovely sound,
A living voice, a breathing harmony,
A bodiless enjoyment—born and dying
With the blest tone which made me !
                                        To be thus—
Grey-hair'd with anguish, like these blasted pines,
Wrecks of a single winter, barkless, branchless,
A blighted trunk upon a cursed root,
Which but supplies a feeling to decay—

And to be thus, eternally but thus,
Having been otherwise! Now furrow'd o'er
With wrinkles, plough'd by moments—not by years,—
And hours, all tortured into ages—hours
Which I outlive!—Ye toppling crags of ice!
Ye avalanches, whom a breath draws down
In mountainous o'erwhelming, come and crush me!
I hear ye momently above, beneath,
Crash with a frequent conflict; but ye pass,
And only fall on things that still would live;
On the young flourishing forest, or the hut
And hamlet of the harmless villager.

From THE SAME.

Manfred.   GLORIOUS Orb! the idol
Of early nature, and the vigorous race
Of undiseased mankind, the giant sons
Of the embrace of angels, with a sex
More beautiful than they, which did draw down
The erring spirits who can ne'er return.—
Most glorious orb! that wert a worship, ere
The mystery of thy making was reveal'd!
Thou earliest minister of the Almighty,
Which gladden'd, on their mountain tops, the hearts

Of the Chaldean shepherds, till they pour'd
Themselves in orisons! Thou material God!
And representative of the Unknown—
Who chose thee for his shadow! Thou chief star!
Centre of many stars! which mak'st our earth
Endurable, and temperest the hues
And hearts of all who walk within thy rays!
Sire of the seasons! Monarch of the climes,
And those who dwell in them! for near or far,
Our inborn spirits have a tint of thee
Even as our outward aspects;—thou dost rise,
And shine, and set in glory. Fare thee well!
I ne'er shall see thee more. As my first glance
Of love and wonder was for thee, then take
My latest look; thou wilt not beam on one
To whom the gifts of life and warmth have been
Of a more fatal nature.

From " *THE PROPHECY OF DANTE.*"

CANTO II.

THE Spirit of the fervent days of Old,
  When words were things that came to pass, and
    thought
  Flash'd o'er the future, bidding men behold
Their children's children's doom already brought
  Forth from the abyss of time which is to be,
  The chaos of events, where lie half-wrought
Shapes that must undergo mortality;
  What the great Seers of Israel wore within,
  That spirit was on them, and is on me,
And if, Cassandra-like, amidst the din
  Of conflict none will hear, or hearing heed
  This voice from out the Wilderness, the sin
Be theirs, and my own feelings be my meed,
  The only guerdon I have ever known.
  Hast thou not bled? and hast thou still to bleed,

Italia? Ah! to me such things, foreshown
With dim sepulchral light, bid me forget
In thine irreparable wrongs my own ;
We can have but one country, and even yet
　　Thou'rt mine—my bones shall be within thy breast,
　　My soul within thy language, which once set
With our old Roman sway in the wide West ;
　　But I will make another tongue arise
　　As lofty and more sweet, in which express'd
The hero's ardour, or the lover's sighs,
　　Shall find alike such sounds for every theme
　　That every word, as brilliant as thy skies,
Shall realise a poet's proudest dream,
　　And make thee Europe's nightingale of song ;
　　So that all present speech to thine shall seem
The note of meaner birds, and every tongue
　　Confess its barbarism when compared with thine.
　　This shalt thou owe to him thou didst so wrong,
Thy Tuscan bard, the banish'd Ghibelline.
　　Woe! woe! the veil of coming centuries
　　Is rent,—a thousand years which yet supine
Lie like the ocean waves ere winds arise,
　　Heaving in dark and sullen undulation,
　　Float from eternity into these eyes ;
The storms yet sleep, the clouds still keep their
　　　　station,

The unborn earthquake yet is in the womb,
The bloody chaos yet expects creation,
But all things are disposing for thy doom ;
The elements await but for the word,
" Let there be darkness !" and thou grow'st a tomb !
Yes ! thou, so beautiful, shalt feel the sword,
Thou, Italy ! so fair that Paradise,
Revived in thee, blooms forth to man restored :
Ah ! must the sons of Adam lose it twice ?
Thou, Italy ! whose ever golden fields,
Plough'd by the sunbeams solely, would suffice
For the world's granary ; thou, whose sky heaven gilds
With brighter stars, and robes with deeper blue ;
Thou, in whose pleasant places Summer builds
Her palace, in whose cradle Empire grew,
And form'd the Eternal City's ornaments
From spoils of kings whom freemen overthrew ;
Birthplace of heroes, sanctuary of saints,
Where earthly first, then heavenly glory made
Her home ; thou, all which fondest fancy paints,
And finds her prior vision but portray'd
In feeble colours, when the eye—from the Alp
Of horrid snow, and rock, and shaggy shade
Of desert-loving pine, whose emerald scalp
Nods to the storm—dilates and dotes o'er thee,
And wistfully implores, as 'twere for help

To see thy sunny fields, my Italy,
  Nearer and nearer yet, and dearer still
  The more approach'd, and dearest were they free,
Thou—thou must wither to each tyrant's will:
  The Goth hath been,—the German, Frank, and Hun
  Are yet to come,—and on the imperial hill
Ruin, already proud of the deeds done
  By the old barbarians, there awaits the new,
  Throned on the Palatine, while lost and won
Rome at her feet lies bleeding; and the hue
  Of human sacrifice and Roman slaughter
  Troubles the clotted air, of late so blue,
And deepens into red the saffron water
  Of Tiber, thick with dead; the helpless priest,
  And still more helpless nor less holy daughter,
Vow'd to their God, have shrieking fled, and ceased
  Their ministry: the nations take their prey,
  Iberian, Almain, Lombard, and the beast
And bird, wolf, vulture, more humane than they
  Are; these but gorge the flesh and lap the gore
  Of the departed, and then go their way;
But those, the human savages, explore
  All paths of torture, and insatiate yet,
  With Ugolino hunger prowl for more.
Nine moons shall rise o'er scenes like this and set;
  The chiefless army of the dead, which late

Beneath the traitor Prince's banner met,
Hath left its leader's ashes at the gate ;
Had but the royal Rebel lived, perchance
Thou hadst been spared, but his involved thy fate.
Oh ! Rome, the spoiler or the spoil of France,
From Brennus to the Bourbon, never, never
Shall foreign standard to thy walls advance,
But Tiber shall become a mournful river.
Oh ! when the strangers pass the Alps and Po,
Crush them, ye rocks ! floods whelm them, and for
ever !
Why sleep the idle avalanches so,
To topple on the lonely pilgrim's head ?
Why doth Eridanus but overflow
The peasant's harvest from his turbid bed ?
Were not each barbarous horde a nobler prey ?
Over Cambyses' host the desert spread
Her sandy ocean, and the sea-waves' sway
Roll'd over Pharaoh and his thousands,—why,
Mountains and waters, do ye not as they ?
And you, ye men ! Romans who dare not die,
Sons of the conquerors who overthrew
Those who o'erthrew proud Xerxes, where yet lie
The dead whose tomb Oblivion never knew,
Are the Alps weaker than Thermopylæ ?
Their passes more alluring to the view

Of an invader ? is it they, or ye,
   That to each host the mountain-gate unbar,
   And leave the march in peace, the passage free ?
Why, Nature's self detains the victor's car,
   And makes your land impregnable, if earth
   Could be so ; but alone she will not war,
Yet aids the warrior worthy of his birth
   In a soil where the mothers bring forth men :
   Not so with those whose souls are little worth ;
For them no fortress can avail,—the den
   Of the poor reptile which preserves its sting
   Is more secure than walls of adamant, when
The hearts of those within are quivering.
   Are ye not brave ?   Yes, yet the Ausonian soil
   Hath hearts, and hands, and arms, and hosts to
      bring
Against Oppression ; but how vain the toil,
   While still Division sows the seeds of woe
   And weakness, till the stranger reaps the spoil !
Oh ! my own beauteous land ! so long laid low,
   So long the grave of thy own children's hopes,
   When there is but required a single blow
To break the chain, yet—yet the Avenger stops,
   And Doubt and Discord step 'twixt thine and thee,
   And join their strength to that which with thee
      copes ;

What is there wanting then to set thee free,
　And show thy beauty in its fullest light?
　To make the Alps impassable ; and we,
Her sons, may do this with *one* deed —— Unite.

From THE SAME.—CANTO IV.

WITHIN the ages which before me pass
　Art shall resume and equal even the sway
　Which with Apelles and old Phidias
She held in Hellas' unforgotten day.
　Ye shall be taught by Ruin to revive
　The Grecian forms at least from their decay,
And Roman souls at last again shall live
　In Roman works wrought by Italian hands,
　And temples, loftier than the old temples, give
New wonders to the world ; and while still stands
　The austere Pantheon, into heaven shall soar
　A dome, its image, while the base expands
Into a fane surpassing all before,
　Such as all flesh shall flock to kneel in : ne'er
　Such sight hath been unfolded by a door
As this, to which all nations shall repair
　And lay their sins at this huge gate of heaven.
　And the bold Architect unto whose care

G

The daring charge to raise it shall be given,
  Whom all hearts shall acknowledge as their lord,
  Whether into the marble chaos driven
His chisel bid the Hebrew, at whose word
  Israel left Egypt, stop the waves in stone,
  Or hues of Hell be by his pencil pour'd
Over the damn'd before the Judgment-throne,
  Such as I saw them, such as all shall see,
  Or fanes be built of grandeur yet unknown,
The stream of his great thoughts shall spring from me,
  The Ghibelline, who traversed the three realms
  Which form the empire of eternity.
Amidst the clash of swords, and clang of helms,
  The age which I anticipate, no less
  Shall be the Age of Beauty, and while whelms,
Calamity the nations with distress,
  The genius of my country shall arise,
  A Cedar towering o'er the Wilderness,
Lovely in all its branches to all eyes,
  Fragrant as fair, and recognised afar,
  Wafting its native incense through the skies.
Sovereigns shall pause amidst their sport of war,
  Wean'd for an hour from blood, to turn and gaze
  On canvas or on stone; and they who mar
All beauty upon earth, compell'd to praise,
  Shall feel the power of that which they destroy;

And Art's mistaken gratitude shall raise
To tyrants who but take her for a toy,
   Emblems and monuments, and prostitute
   Her charms to pontiffs proud, who but employ
The man of genius as the meanest brute
   To bear a burthen, and to serve a need,
   To sell his labours, and his soul to boot.
Who toils for nations may be poor indeed,
   But free; who sweats for monarchs is no more
   Than the gilt chamberlain, who, clothed and fee'd,
Stands sleek and slavish, bowing at his door.

THE VISION OF JUDGMENT.

SAINT PETER sat by the celestial gate :
  His keys were rusty, and the lock was dull,
So little trouble had been given of late ;
  Not that the place by any means was full,
But since the Gallic era " eighty-eight "
  The devils had ta'en a longer, stronger pull,
And " a pull altogether," as they say
At sea—which drew most souls another way.

The angels all were singing out of tune,
  And hoarse with having little else to do,
Excepting to wind up the sun and moon,
  Or curb a runaway young star or two,
Or wild colt of a comet, which too soon
  Broke out of bounds o'er th' ethereal blue,
Splitting some planet with its playful tail,
As boats are sometimes by a wanton whale.

The guardian seraphs had retired on high,
    Finding their charges past all care below;
Terrestrial business fill'd nought in the sky
    Save the recording angel's black bureau;
Who found, indeed, the facts to multiply
    With such rapidity of vice and woe,
That he had stripp'd off both his wings in quills,
And yet was in arrear of human ills.

His business so augmented of late years,
    That he was forced, against his will no doubt,
(Just like those cherubs, earthly ministers,)
    For some resource to turn himself about,
And claim the help of his celestial peers,
    To aid him ere he should be quite worn out
By the increased demand for his remarks:
Six angels and twelve saints were named his clerks.

This was a handsome board—at least for heaven;
    And yet they had even then enough to do,
So many conquerors' cars were daily driven,
    So many kingdoms fitted up anew;
Each day too slew its thousands six or seven,
    Till at the crowning carnage, Waterloo,
They threw their pens down in divine disgust—
The page was so besmear'd with blood and dust.

This by the way ; 'tis not mine to record
    What angels shrink from : even the very devil
On this occasion his own work abhorr'd,
    So surfeited with the infernal revel :
Though he himself had sharpen'd every sword,
    It almost quench'd his innate thirst of evil.
(Here Satan's sole good work deserves insertion—
'Tis, that he has both generals in reversion.)

Let's skip a few short years of hollow peace,
    Which peopled earth no better, hell as wont,
And heaven none—they form the tyrant's lease,
    With nothing but new names subscribed upon 't ;
'Twill one day finish : meantime they increase,
    " With seven heads and ten horns," and all in front,
Like Saint John's foretold beast ; but ours are born
Less formidable in the head than horn.

In the first year of freedom's second dawn
    Died George the Third ; although no tyrant, one
Who shielded tyrants, till each sense withdrawn
    Left him nor mental nor external sun :
A better farmer ne'er brush'd dew from lawn,
    A worse king never left a realm undone !
He died—but left his subjects still behind,
One half as mad—and t'other no less blind.

He died ! his death made no great stir on earth :
His burial made some pomp ; there was profusion
Of velvet, gilding, brass, and no great dearth
Of aught but tears—save those shed by collusion.
For these things may be bought at their true worth ;
Of elegy there was the due infusion—
Bought also ; and the torches, cloaks, and banners,
Heralds, and relics of old Gothic manners,

Form'd a sepulchral melodrame.   Of all
The fools who flock'd to swell or see the show,
Who cared about the corpse ?   The funeral
Made the attraction, and the black the woe.   [pall ;
There throbb'd not there a thought which pierced the
And when the gorgeous coffin was laid low,
It seem'd the mockery of hell to fold
The rottenness of eighty years in gold.

So mix his body with the dust !   It might
Return to what it *must* far sooner, were
The natural compound left alone to fight
Its way back into earth, and fire, and air ;
But the unnatural balsams merely blight
What nature made him at his birth, as bare
As the mere million's base unmummied clay—
Yet all his spices but prolong decay.

He's dead—and upper earth with him has done ;
  He's buried ; save the undertaker's bill,
Or lapidary scrawl, the world is gone
  For him, unless he left a German will :
But where's the proctor who will ask his son ?
  In whom his qualities are reigning still,
Except that household virtue, most uncommon,
Of constancy to a bad, ugly woman.

" God save the king ! "   It is a large economy
  In God to save the like ; but if he will
Be saving, all the better ; for not one am I
  Of those who think damnation better still :
I hardly know too if not quite alone am I
  In this small hope of bettering future ill
By circumscribing, with some slight restriction,
The eternity of hell's hot jurisdiction.

I know this is unpopular ; I know
  'Tis blasphemous ; I know one may be damn'd
For hoping no one else may e'er be so ;
  I know my catechism ; I know we're cramm'd
With the best doctrines till we quite o'erflow ;
  I know that all save England's church have shamm'd,
And that the other twice two hundred churches
And synagogues have made a *damn'd* bad purchase.

God help us all! God help me too! I am,
  God knows, as helpless as the devil can wish,
And not a whit more difficult to damn,
  Than is to bring to land a late-hook'd fish,
Or to the butcher to purvey the lamb ;
  Not that I'm 'fit for such a noble dish,
As one day will be that immortal fry
Of almost everybody born to die.

Saint Peter sat by the celestial gate,
  And nodded o'er his keys ; when, lo ! there came
A wondrous noise he had not heard of late—
  A rushing sound of wind, and stream, and flame ;
In short, a roar of things extremely great,
  Which would have made aught save a saint exclaim;
But he, with first a start and then a wink,
Said, " There's another star gone out, I think ! "

But ere he could return to his repose,
  A cherub flapp'd his right wing o'er his eyes—
At which Saint Peter yawn'd, and rubb'd his nose :
  " Saint porter," said the angel, " prithee rise ! "
Waving a goodly wing, which glow'd, as glows
  An earthly peacock's tail, with heavenly dyes :
To which the saint replied, " Well, what's the matter ?
Is Lucifer come back with all this clatter ? "

" No," quoth the cherub; "George the Third is dead."
"And who *is* George the Third?" replied the apostle:
" *What George? what Third?*" "The king of England,"
The angel. "Well! he won't find kings to jostle [said
Him on his way ; but does he wear his head ?
Because the last we saw here had a tustle,
And ne'er would have got into heaven's good graces,
Had he not flung his head in all our faces.

" He was, if I remember, king of France ;
That head of his, which could not keep a crown
On earth, yet ventured in my face to advance
A claim to those of martyrs—like my own :
If I had had my sword, as I had once
When I cut ears off, I had cut him down ;
But having but my *keys*, and not my brand,
I only knock'd his head from out his hand.

" And then he set up such a headless howl,
That all the saints came out and took him in ;
And there he sits by Saint Paul, cheek by jowl ;
That fellow Paul—the parvenù ! The skin
Of Saint Bartholomew, which makes his cowl
In heaven, and upon earth redeem'd his sin,
So as to make a martyr, never sped
Better than did this weak and wooden head.

" But had it come up here upon its shoulders,
    There would have been a different tale to tell :
The fellow-feeling in the saints beholders
    Seems to have acted on them like a spell ;
And so this very foolish head heaven solders
    Back on its trunk : it may be very well,
And seems the custom here to overthrow
Whatever has been wisely done below."

The angel answer'd, " Peter ! do not pout :
    The king who comes has head and all entire,
And never knew much what it was about—
    He did as doth the puppet—by its wire,
And will be judged like all the rest, no doubt :
    My business and your own is not to inquire
Into such matters, but to mind our cue—
Which is to act as we are bid to do."

While thus they spake, the angelic caravan,
    Arriving like a rush of mighty wind,
Cleaving the fields of space, as doth the swan
    Some silver stream (say Ganges, Nile, or Inde,
Or Thames, or Tweed), and 'midst them an old man
    With an old soul, and both extremely blind,
Halted before the gate, and in his shroud
Seated their fellow traveller on a cloud.

But bringing up the rear of this bright host
  A Spirit of a different aspect waved
His wings, like thunder-clouds above some coast
  Whose barren beach with frequent wrecks is paved ;
His brow was like the deep when tempest-toss'd ;
  Fierce and unfathomable thoughts engraved
Eternal wrath on his immortal face,
And *where* he gazed a gloom pervaded space.

As he drew near, he gazed upon the gate
  Ne'er to be enter'd more by him or Sin,
With such a glance of supernatural hate,
  As made Saint Peter wish himself within ;
He patter'd with his keys at a great rate,
  And sweated through his apostolic skin :
Of course his perspiration was but ichor,
Or some such other spiritual liquor.

The very cherubs huddled all together,
  Like birds when soars the falcon ; and they felt
A tingling to the tip of every feather,
  And form'd a circle like Orion's belt   [whither
Around their poor old charge ; who scarce knew
  His guards had led him, though they gently dealt
With royal manes (for by many stories,
And true, we learn the angels all are Tories).

As things were in this posture, the gate flew
   Asunder, and the flashing of its hinges
Flung over space an universal hue
   Of many-colour'd flame, until its tinges
Reach'd even our speck of earth, and made a new
   Aurora borealis spread its fringes
O'er the North Pole ; the same seen, when ice-bound,
By Captain Parry's crew, in " Melville's Sound."

And from the gate thrown open issued beaming
   A beautiful and mighty Thing of Light,
Radiant with glory, like a banner streaming
   Victorious from some world-o'erthrowing fight :
My poor comparisons must needs be teeming
   With earthly likenesses, for here the night
Of clay obscures our best conceptions, saving
Johanna Southcote, or Bob Southey raving.

'Twas the archangel Michael ; all men know
   The make of angels and archangels, since
There's scarce a scribbler has not one to show,
   From the fiends' leader to the angels' prince ;
There also are some altar-pieces, though
   I really can't say that they much evince
One's inner notions of immortal spirits ;
But let the connoisseurs explain *their* merits.

Michael flew forth in glory and in good ;
  A goodly work of him from whom all glory
And good arise ; the portal past—he stood ;
  Before him the young cherubs and saints hoary—
(I say *young*, begging to be understood
  By looks, not years ; and should be very sorry
To state, they were not older than St. Peter,
But merely that they seem'd a little sweeter).

The cherubs and the saints bow'd down before
  That arch-angelic hierarch, the first
Of essences angelical, who wore
  The aspect of a god ; but this ne'er nursed
Pride in his heavenly bosom, in whose core
  No thought, save for his Master's service, durst
Intrude, however glorified and high ;
He knew him but the viceroy of the sky.

He and the sombre, silent Spirit met—
  They knew each other both for good and ill ;
Such was their power, that neither could forget
  His former friend and future foe ; but still
There was a high, immortal, proud regret
  In either's eye, as if 'twere less their will
Than destiny to make the eternal years
Their date of war, and their "champ clos" the spheres.

But here they were in neutral space : we know
From Job, that Satan hath the power to pay
A heavenly visit thrice a year or so ;
And that the "sons of God," like those of clay,
Must keep him company ; and we might show
From the same book, in how polite a way
The dialogue is held between the Powers
Of Good and Evil—but 'twould take up hours.

And this is not a theologic tract,
To prove with Hebrew and with Arabic,
If Job be allegory or a fact,
But a true narrative ; and thus I pick
From out the whole but such and such an act
As sets aside the slightest thought of trick.
'Tis every tittle true, beyond suspicion,
And accurate as any other vision.

The spirits were in neutral space, before
The gate of heaven ; like eastern thresholds is
The place where Death's grand cause is argued o'er,
And souls despatch'd to that world or to this ;
And therefore Michael and the other wore
A civil aspect : though they did not kiss,
Yet still between his Darkness and his Brightness
There pass'd a mutual glance of great politeness.

The Archangel bow'd, not like a modern beau,
   But with a graceful Oriental bend,
Pressing one radiant arm just where below
   The heart in good men is supposed to tend;
He turn'd as to an equal, not too low,
   But kindly; Satan met his ancient friend
With more hauteur, as might an old Castilian
Poor noble meet a mushroom rich civilian.

He merely bent his diabolic brow
   An instant; and then raising it, he stood
In act to assert his right or wrong, and show
   Cause why King George by no means could or should
Make out a case to be exempt from woe
   Eternal, more than other kings, endued
With better sense and hearts, whom history mentions,
Who long have "paved hell with their good intentions."

Michael began: "What wouldst thou with this man,
   Now dead, and brought before the Lord? What ill
Hath he wrought since his mortal race began,
   That thou canst claim him? Speak! and do thy will,
If it be just: if in this earthly span
   He hath been greatly failing to fulfil
His duties as a king and mortal, say,
And he is thine; if not, let him have way."

"Michael!" replied the Prince of Air, "even here,
 Before the Gate of him thou servest, must
I claim my subject: and will make appear
 That as he was my worshipper in dust,
So shall he be in spirit, although dear
 To thee and thine, because nor wine nor lust
Were of his weaknesses; yet on the throne
He reign'd o'er millions to serve me alone.

"Look to *our* earth, or rather *mine*; it was,
 Once, more thy master's: but I triumph not
At this poor planet's conquest; nor, alas!
 Need he thou servest envy me my lot:
With all the myriads of bright worlds which pass
 In worship round him, he may have forgot
Yon weak creation of such paltry things:
I think few worth damnation save their kings,—

"And these but as a kind of quit-rent, to
 Assert my right as lord: and even had
I such an inclination, 'twere (as you
 Well know) superfluous; they are grown so bad,
That hell has nothing better left to do
 Than leave them to themselves: so much more mad
And evil by their own internal curse,
Heaven cannot make them better, nor I worse.

H

" Look to the earth, I said, and say again :
    When this old, blind, mad, helpless, weak, poor worm
Began in youth's first bloom and flush to reign,
    The world and he both wore a different form,
And much of earth and all the watery plain
    Of ocean call'd him king : through many a storm
His isles had floated on the abyss of time ;
For the rough virtues chose them for their clime.

" He came to his sceptre young ; he leaves it old :
    Look to the state in which he found his realm,
And left it ; and his annals too behold,
    How to a minion first he gave the helm ;
How grew upon his heart a thirst for gold,
    The beggar's vice, which can but overwhelm
The meanest hearts ; and for the rest, but glance
Thine eye along America and France.

" 'Tis true, he was a tool from first to last
    (I have the workmen safe) ; but as a tool
So let him be consumed.   From out the past
    Of ages, since mankind have known the rule
Of monarchs—from the bloody rolls amass'd
    Of sin and slaughter—from the Cæsar's school,
Take the worst pupil ; and produce a reign
More drench'd with gore, more cumber'd with the slain.

" He ever warr'd with freedom and the free :
    Nations as men, home subjects, foreign foes,
So that they utter'd the word 'Liberty !'
    Found George the Third their first opponent. Whose
History was ever stain'd as his will be
    With national and individual woes ?
I grant his household abstinence ; I grant
His neutral virtues, which most monarchs want ;

" I know he was a constant consort ; own
    He was a decent sire, and middling lord.
All this is much, and most upon a throne ;
    As temperance, if at Apicius' board,
Is more than at an anchorite's supper shown.
    I grant him all the kindest can accord ;
And this was well for him, but not for those
Millions who found him what oppression chose.

" The New World shook him off; the Old yet groans
    Beneath what he and his prepared, if not
Completed : he leaves heirs on many thrones
    To all his vices, without what begot
Compassion for him—his tame virtues ; drones
    Who sleep, or despots who have now forgot
A lesson which shall be re-taught them, wake
Upon the thrones of earth ; but let them quake !

" Five millions of the primitive, who hold
    The faith which makes ye great on earth, implored
A *part* of that vast *all* they held of old,—
    Freedom to worship—not alone your Lord,
Michael, but you, and you, Saint Peter !   Cold
    Must be your souls, if you have not abhorr'd
The foe to Catholic participation
In all the license of a Christian nation.

" True ! he allow'd them to pray God ; but as
    A consequence of prayer, refused the law
Which would have placed them upon the same base
    With those who did not hold the saints in awe."
But here Saint Peter started from his place,
    And cried, " You may the prisoner withdraw :
Ere heaven shall ope her portals to this Guelph,
While I am guard, may I be damn'd myself !

" Sooner will I with Cerberus exchange
    My office (and *his* is no sinecure)
Than see this royal Bedlam bigot range
    The azure fields of heaven, of that be sure ! "
" Saint ! " replied Satan, " you do well to avenge
    The wrongs he made your satellites endure ;
And if to this exchange you should be given,
I'll try to coax *our* Cerberus up to heaven ! "

Here Michael interposed : "Good saint! and devil!
Pray, not so fast; you both outrun discretion.
Saint Peter! you were wont to be more civil!
Satan! excuse this warmth of his expression,
And condescension to the vulgar's level :
Even saints sometimes forget themselves in session.
Have you got more to say?"—"No."—"If you please,
I'll trouble you to call your witnesses."

Then Satan turn'd and waved his swarthy hand,
Which stirr'd with its electric qualities
Clouds farther off than we can understand,
Although we find him sometimes in our skies;
Infernal thunder shook both sea and land
In all the planets, and hell's batteries
Let off the artillery, which Milton mentions
As one of Satan's most sublime inventions.

This was a signal unto such damn'd souls
As have the privilege of their damnation
Extended far beyond the mere controls
Of worlds past, present, or to come ; no station
Is theirs particularly in the rolls
Of hell assign'd ; but where their inclination
Or business carries them in search of game,
They may range freely— being damn'd the same.

They're proud of this—as very well they may,
　It being a sort of knighthood, or gilt key
Stuck in their loins ; or like to an "entré"
　Up the back stairs, or such free-masonry.
I borrow my comparisons from clay,
　Being clay myself.   Let not those spirits be
Offended with such base low likenesses ;
We know their posts are nobler far than these.

When the great signal ran from heaven to hell—
　About ten million times the distance reckon'd
From our sun to its earth, as we can tell
　How much time it takes up, even to a second,
For every ray that travels to dispel
　The fogs of London, through which, dimly beacon'd,
The weathercocks are gilt some thrice a year,
If that the *summer* is not too severe :

I say that I can tell—'twas half a minute ;
　I know the solar beams take up more time
Ere, pack'd up for their journey, they begin it ;
　But then their telegraph is less sublime,
And if they ran a race, they would not win it
　'Gainst Satan's couriers bound for their own clime.
The sun takes up some years for every ray
To reach its goal—the devil not half a day.

Upon the verge of space, about the size
　Of half-a-crown, a little speck appear'd
(I've seen a something like it in the skies
　In the Ægean, ere a squall) ; it near'd,
And, growing bigger, took another guise ;
　Like an aërial ship it tack'd, and steer'd,
Or *was* steer'd (I am doubtful of the grammar
Of the last phrase, which makes the stanza stammer ;—

But take your choice) : and then it grew a cloud ;
　And so it was—a cloud of witnesses.
But such a cloud !　No land e'er saw a crowd
　Of locusts numerous as the heavens saw these ;
They shadow'd with their myriads space ; their loud
　And varied cries were like those of wild geese
(If nations may be liken'd to a goose),
And realised the phrase of " hell broke loose."

Here crash'd a sturdy oath of stout John Bull,
　Who damn'd away his eyes as heretofore : [wull ? "
There　Paddy brogued " By Jasus ! "—" What's your
　The temperate Scot exclaim'd : the French ghost
In certain terms I shan't translate in full,　　[swore
　As the first coachman will ; and 'midst the war,
The voice of Jonathan was heard to express,
" *Our* president is going to war, I guess."

Besides there were the Spaniard, Dutch, and Dane;
  In short, an universal shoal of shades,
From Otaheite's isle to Salisbury Plain,
  Of all climes and professions, years and trades,
Ready to swear against the good king's reign,
  Bitter as clubs in cards are against spades:
All summon'd by this grand "subpœna," to
Try if kings mayn't be damn'd like me or you.

When Michael saw this host, he first grew pale,
  As angels can; next, like Italian twilight,
He turn'd all colours—as a peacock's tail,
  Or sunset streaming through a Gothic skylight
In some old abbey, or a trout not stale,
  Or distant lightning on the horizon *by* night,
Or a fresh rainbow, or a grand review
Of thirty regiments in red, green, and blue.

Then he address'd himself to Satan: "Why—
  My good old friend, for such I deem you, though
Our different parties make us fight so shy,
  I ne'er mistake you for a *personal* foe;
Our difference is *political*, and I
  Trust that, whatever may occur below,
You know my great respect for you: and this
Makes me regret whate'er you do amiss—

"Why, my dear Lucifer, would you abuse
  My call for witnesses? I did not mean
That you should half of earth and hell produce;
  'Tis even superfluous, since two honest, clean,
True testimonies are enough: we lose
  Our time, nay, our eternity, between
The accusation and defence: if we
Hear both, 'twill stretch our immortality."

Satan replied, "To me the matter is
  Indifferent, in a personal point of view:
I can have fifty better souls than this
  With far less trouble than we have gone through
Already; and I merely argued his
  Late majesty of Britain's case with you
Upon a point of form: you may dispose
Of him; I've kings enough below, God knows!"

Thus spoke the Demon (late call'd "multifaced"
  By multo-scribbling Southey). "Then we'll call
One or two persons of the myriads placed
  Around our congress, and dispense with all
The rest," quoth Michael: "Who may be so graced
  As to speak first? there's choice enough—who shall
It be?" Then Satan answer'd, "There are many;
But you may choose Jack Wilkes as well as any."

A merry, cock-eyed, curious-looking sprite
   Upon the instant started from the throng,
Dress'd in a fashion now forgotten quite ;
   For all the fashions of the flesh stick long
By people ín the next world ; where unite
   All the costumes since Adam's, right or wrong,
From Eve's fig-leaf down to the petticoat,
Almost as scanty, of days less remote.

The spirit look'd around upon the crowds
   Assembled, and exclaim'd, " My friends of all
The spheres, we shall catch cold amongst these clouds;
   So let's to business : why this general call ?
If those are freeholders I see in shrouds,
   And 'tis for an election that they bawl,
Behold a candidate with unturn'd coat !
Saint Peter, may I count upon your vote ?"

" Sir," replied Michael, " you mistake ; these things
   Are of a former life, and what we do
Above is more august ; to judge of kings
   Is the tribunal met : so now you know."
" Then I presume those gentlemen with wings,"
   Said Wilkes, " are cherubs ; and that soul below
Looks much like George the Third, but to my mind
A good deal older—Bless me ! is he blind ?"

" He is what you behold him, and his doom
 Depends upon his deeds," the Angel said ;
" If you have aught to arraign in him, the tomb
 Gives license to the humblest beggar's head
To lift itself against the loftiest."—" Some,"
 Said Wilkes, " don't wait to see them laid in lead,
For such a liberty—and I, for one,
Have told them what I thought beneath the sun."

"*Above* the sun repeat, then, what thou hast
 To urge against him," said the Archangel.   " Why,"
Replied the spirit, " since old scores are past,
 Must I turn evidence?   In faith, not I.
Besides, I beat him hollow at the last,
 With all his Lords and Commons: in the sky
I don't like ripping up old stories, since
His conduct was but natural in a prince.

" Foolish, no doubt, and wicked, to oppress
 A poor unlucky devil without a shilling ;
But then I blame the man himself much less
 Than Bute and Grafton, and shall be unwilling
To see him punish'd here for their excess,
 Since they were both damn'd long ago, and still in
Their place below: for me, I have forgiven,
And vote his ' habeas corpus ' into heaven."

"Wilkes," said the Devil, "I understand all this;
   You turn'd to half a courtier ere you died,
And seem to think it would not be amiss
   To grow a whole one on the other side
Of Charon's ferry; you forget that *his*
   Reign is concluded; whatsoe'er betide,
He won't be sovereign more: you've lost your labour,
For at the best he will but be your neighbour.

"However, I knew what to think of it,
   When I beheld you in your jesting way,
Flitting and whispering round about the spit
   Where Belial, upon duty for the day, ·
With Fox's lard was basting William Pitt,
   His pupil; I knew what to think, I say:
That fellow even in hell breeds farther ills;
I'll have him *gagg'd*—'twas one of his own bills.

"Call Junius!" From the crowd a shadow stalk'd,
   And at the name there was a general squeeze,
So that the very ghosts no longer walk'd
   In comfort, at their own aërial ease,
But were all ramm'd, and jamm'd (but to be balk'd,
   As we shall see), and jostled hands and knees,
Like wind compress'd and pent within a bladder,
Or like a human colic, which is sadder.

The shadow came—a tall, thin, grey-hair'd figure,
  That look'd as it had been a shade on earth;
Quick in its motions, with an air of vigour,
  But nought to mark its breeding or its birth;
Now it wax'd little, then again grew bigger,
  With now an air of gloom, or savage mirth;
But as you gazed upon its features, they
Changed every instant—to *what*, none could say.

The more intently the ghosts gazed, the less
  Could they distinguish whose the features were;
The Devil himself seem'd puzzled even to guess;
  They varied like a dream—now here, now there;
And several people swore from out the press,
  They knew him perfectly; and one could swear
He was his father: upon which another
Was sure he was his mother's cousin's brother:

Another, that he was a duke, or knight,
  An orator, a lawyer, or a priest,
A nabob, a man-midwife; but the wight
  Mysterious changed his countenance at least
As oft as they their minds; though in full sight
  He stood, the puzzle only was increased;
The man was a phantasmagoria in
Himself—he was so volatile and thin.

The moment that you had pronounced him *one*,
   Presto ! his face changed, and he was another ;
And when that change was hardly well put on,
   It varied, till I don't think his own mother
(If that he had a mother) would her son
   Have known, he shifted so from one to t'other ;
Till guessing from a pleasure grew a task,
At this epistolary " Iron Mask."

For sometimes he like Cerberus would seem—
   " Three gentlemen at once " (as sagely says
Good Mrs. Malaprop) ; then you might deem
   That he was not even *one;* now many rays
Were flashing round him; and now a thick steam
   Hid him from sight—like fogs on London days :
Now Burke, now Tooke, he grew to people's fancies,
And certes often like Sir Philip Francis.

I've an hypothesis—'tis quite my own ;
   I never let it out till now, for fear
Of doing people harm about the throne,
   And injuring some minister or peer,
On whom the stigma might perhaps be blown ;
   It is—my gentle public, lend thine ear !
'Tis, that what Junius we are wont to call
Was *really, truly*, nobody at all.

I don't see wherefore letters should not be
  Written without hands, since we daily view
Them written without heads; and books, we see,
  Are fill'd as well without the latter too:
And really till we fix on somebody
  For certain sure to claim them as his due,
Their author, like the Niger's mouth, will bother
The world to say if *there* be mouth or author.

"And who and what art thou?" the Archangel said.
  "For *that* you may consult my title-page,"
Replied this mighty shadow of a shade:
  "If I have kept my secret half an age,
I scarce shall tell it now."—"Canst thou upbraid,"
  Continued Michael, "George Rex, or allege
Aught further?" Junius answer'd, "You had better
First ask him for *his* answer to my letter:

"My charges upon record will outlast
  The brass of both his epitaph and tomb.
"Repent'st thou not," said Michael, "of some past
  Exaggeration? something which may doom
Thyself if false, as him if true? Thou wast
  Too bitter—is it not so?—in thy gloom
Of passion?"—"Passion!" cried the phantom dim,
"I loved my country, and I hated him.

"What I have written, I have written : let
  The rest be on his head or mine !" So spoke
Old "Nominis Umbra ;" and while speaking yet,
  Away he melted in celestial smoke.
Then Satan said to Michael, "Don't forget
  To call George Washington, and John Horne Tooke,
And Franklin ; "—but at this time there was heard
A cry for room, though not a phantom stirr'd.

At length with jostling, elbowing, and the aid
  Of cherubim appointed to that post,
The devil Asmodeus to the circle made
  His way, and look'd as if his journey cost
Some trouble.   When his burden down he laid,
  "What's this ?" cried Michael ; "why, 'tis not a
"I know it," quoth the incubus ; "but he   [ghost?'
Shall be one, if you leave the affair to me.

"Confound the renegado !   I have sprain'd
  My left wing, he's so heavy ; one would think
Some of his works about his neck were chain'd.
  But to the point ; while hovering o'er the brink
Of Skiddaw (where as usual it still rain'd),
  I saw a taper, far below me, wink,
And stooping, caught this fellow at a libel—
No less on history than the Holy Bible.

" The former is the devil's scripture, and
    The latter yours, good Michael : so the affair
Belongs to all of us, you understand.
    I snatch'd him up just as you see him there,
And brought him off for sentence out of hand :
    I've scarcely been ten minutes in the air—
At least a quarter it can hardly be :   .
I dare say that his wife is still at tea."

Here Satan said, " I know this man of old,
    And have expected him for some time here ;
A sillier fellow you will scarce behold,
    Or more conceited in his petty sphere :
But surely it was not worth while to fòld
    Such trash below your wing, Asmodeus dear :
We had the poor wretch safe (without being bored
With carriage) coming of his own accord.

" But since he's here, let's see what he has done."
    " Done ! " cried Asmodeus, " he anticipates
The very business you are now upon,
    And scribbles as if head clerk to the Fates.
Who knows to what his ribaldry may run,
    When such an ass as this, like Balaam's, prates ? "
" Let's hear," quoth Michael, " what he has to say :
You know we're bound to that in every way."

Now the bard, glad to get an audience, which
    By no means often was his case below,
Began to cough, and hawk, and hem, and pitch
    His voice into that awful note of woe
To all unhappy hearers within reach
    Of poets when the tide of rhyme's in flow ;
But stuck fast with his first hexameter,
Not one of all whose gouty feet would stir.

But ere the spavin'd dactyls could be spurr'd
    Into recitative, in great dismay
Both cherubim and seraphim were heard
    To murmur loudly through their long array ;
And Michael rose ere he could get a word
    Of all his founder'd verses under way,   [best—
And cried, " For God's sake stop, my friend ! 'twere
Non Di, non homines—you know the rest."

A general bustle spread throughout the throng,
    Which seem'd to hold all verse in detestation ;
The angels had of course enough of song
    When upon service ; and the generation
Of ghosts had heard too much in life, not long
    Before, to profit by a new occasion :
The monarch, mute till then, exclaim'd, " What ! what !
Pye come again ?   No more—no more of that ! "

The tumult grew; an universal cough
  Convulsed the skies, as during a debate,
When Castlereagh has been up long enough
  (Before he was first minister of state,
I mean—the *slaves hear now*); some cried "Off, off!"
  As at a farce; till, grown quite desperate,
The bard Saint Peter pray'd to interpose
(Himself an author) only for his prose.

The varlet was not an ill-favour'd knave;
  A good deal like a vulture in the face,
With a hook nose and a hawk's eye, which gave
  A smart and sharper-looking sort of grace
To his whole aspect, which, though rather grave,
  Was by no means so ugly as his case;
But that, indeed, was hopeless as can be,
Quite a poetic felony " *de se.*"

Then Michael blew his trump, and still'd the noise
  With one still greater, as is yet the mode
On earth besides; except some grumbling voice,
  Which now and then will make a slight inroad
Upon decorous silence, few will twice
  Lift up their lungs when fairly overcrow'd;
And now the bard could plead his own bad cause,
With all the attitudes of self-applause.

1 2

He said—(I only give the heads)—he said,
  He meant no harm in scribbling ; 'twas his way
Upon all topics ; 'twas, besides, his bread,
  Of which he butter'd both sides ; 'twould delay
Too long the assembly (he was pleased to dread),
  And take up rather more time than a day,
To name his works—he would but cite a few—
"Wat Tyler"—"Rhymes on Blenheim"—"Waterloo."

He had written praises of a regicide ;
  He had written praises of all kings whatever ;
He had written for republics far and wide,
  And then against them bitterer than ever ;
For pantisocracy he once had cried
  Aloud, a scheme less moral than 'twas clever ;
Then grew a hearty anti-jacobin—
Had turn'd his coat—and would have turn'd his skin.

He had sung against all battles, and again
  In their high praise and glory ; he had call'd
Reviewing "the ungentle craft," and then
  Become as base a critic as e'er crawl'd—
Fed, paid, and pamper'd by the very men
  By whom his muse and morals had been maul'd :
He had written much blank verse, and blanker prose,
And more of both than anybody knows.

He had written Wesley's life :—here turning round
　To Satan, " Sir, I'm ready to write yours,
In two octavo volumes, nicely bound,
　With notes and preface, all that most allures
The pious purchaser ; and there's no ground
　For fear, for I can choose my own reviewers :
So let me have the proper documents,
That I may add you to my other saints."

Satan bow'd, and was silent. " Well, if you,
　With amiable modesty, decline
My offer, what says Michael ?　There are few
　Whose memoirs could be render'd more divine.
Mine is a pen of all work ; not so new
　As it was once, but I would make you shine
Like your own trumpet.　By the way, my own
Has more of brass in it, and is as well blown.

" But talking about trumpets, here's my Vision !
　Now you shall judge, all people ; yes, you shall
Judge with my judgment, and by my decision
　Be guided who shall enter heaven or fall.
I settle all these things by intuition,
　Times present, past, to come, heaven, hell, and all,
Like King Alfonso.　When I thus see double,
I save the Deity some worlds of trouble."

He ceased, and drew forth an MS. ; and no
    Persuasion on the part of devils, saints,
Or angels, now could stop the torrent ; so
    He read the first three lines of the contents ;
But at the fourth, the whole spiritual show
    Had vanish'd, with variety of scents,
Ambrosial and sulphureous, as they sprang,
Like lightning, off from his " melodious twang."

Those grand heroics acted as a spell :
    The angels stopp'd their ears and plied their pinions ;
The devils ran howling, deafen'd, down to hell ;
    The ghosts fled, gibbering, for their own dominions—
(For 'tis not yet decided where they dwell,
    And I leave every man to his opinions) ;
Michael took refuge in his trump—but, lo !
His teeth were set on edge, he could not blow !

Saint Peter, who has hitherto been known
    For an impetuous saint, upraised his keys,
And at the fifth line knock'd the poet down ;
    Who fell like Phaeton, but more at ease,
Into his lake, for there he did not drown ;
    A different web being by the Destinies
Woven for the Laureate's final wreath, whene'er
Reform shall happen either here or there.

He first sank to the bottom—like his works,
　But soon rose to the surface—like himself;
For all corrupted things are buoy'd like corks,
　By their own rottenness, light as an elf,
Or wisp that flits o'er a morass : he lurks,
　It may be, still, like dull books on a shelf,
In his own den, to scrawl some " Life " or " Vision,"
As Welborn says—" the devil turn'd precisian."

As for the rest, to come to the conclusion
　Of this true dream, the telescope is gone
Which kept my optics free from all delusion,
　And show'd me what I in my turn have shown ;
All I saw farther, in the last confusion,
　Was, that King George slipp'd into heaven for one ;
And when the tumult dwindled to a calm,
I left him practising the hundredth psalm.

From "*DON JUAN.*"

Canto I.

" THEY tell me 'tis decided you depart :
. 'Tis wise—'tis well, but not the less a pain ;
I have no further claim on your young heart,
    Mine is the victim, and would be again :
To love too much has been the only art
    I used ;—I write in haste, and if a stain
Be on this sheet, 'tis not what it appears ;
My eyeballs burn and throb, but have no tears.

" I loved, I love you, for this love have lost
    State, station, heaven, mankind's, my own esteem,
And yet cannot regret what it hath cost,
    So dear is still the memory of that dream ;
Yet, if I name my guilt, 'tis not to boast,
    None can deem harshlier of me than I deem :
I trace this scrawl because I cannot rest—
I've nothing to reproach or to request.

" Man's love is of man's life a thing apart,
   'Tis woman's whole existence; man may range
The court, camp, church, the vessel, and the mart;
   Sword, gown, gain, glory, offer in exchange
Pride, fame, ambition, to fill up his heart,
   And few there are whom these cannot estrange;
Men have all these resources, we but one,
To love again, and be again undone.

" You will proceed in pleasure, and in pride,
   Beloved and loving many; all is o'er
For me on earth, except some years to hide
   My shame and sorrow deep in my heart's core :
These I could bear, but cannot cast aside
   The passion which still rages as before,—
And so farewell—forgive me, love me—No,
That word is idle now—but let it go.

" My breast has been all weakness, is so yet;
  · But still I think I can collect my mind;
My blood still rushes where my spirit's set,
   As roll the waves before the settled wind;
My heart is feminine, nor can forget—
   To all, except one image, madly blind;
So shakes the needle, and so stands the pole,
As vibrates my fond heart to my fix'd soul.

" I have no more to say, but linger still,
   And dare not set my seal upon this sheet,
And yet I may as well the task fulfil,
   My misery can scarce be more complete :
I had not lived till now, could sorrow kill ;   [meet,
   Death shuns the wretch who fain the blow would
And I must even survive this last adieu,
And bear with life, to love and pray for you ! "

From THE SAME.—CANTO II.

THE ship, call'd the most holy " Trinidada,"
   Was steering duly for the port Leghorn ;
For there the Spanish family Moncada
   Were settled long ere Juan's sire was born :
They were relations, and for them he had a
   Letter of introduction, which the morn
Of his departure had been sent him by
His Spanish friends for those in Italy.

His suite consisted of three servants and
   A tutor, the licentiate Pedrillo,
Who several languages did understand,
   But now lay sick and speechless on his pillow,
And, rocking in his hammock, long'd for land,
   His headache being increased by every billow ;
And the waves oozing through the port-hole made
His berth a little damp, and him afraid.

'Twas not without some reason, for the wind
  Increased at night, until it blew a gale ;
And though 'twas not much to a naval mind,
  Some landsmen would have look'd a little pale,
For sailors are, in fact, a different kind :
  At sunset they began to take in sail,
For the sky show'd it would come on to blow,
And carry away, perhaps, a mast or so.

At one o'clock the wind with sudden shift
  Threw the ship right into the trough of the sea,
Which struck her aft, and made an awkward rift,
  Started the stern-post, also shatter'd the
Whole of her stern-frame, and, ere she could lift
  Herself from out her present jeopardy,
The rudder tore away : 'twas time to sound
The pumps, and there were four feet water found.

One gang of people instantly was put
  Upon the pumps, and the remainder set
.To get up part of the cargo, and what not ;
  But they could not come at the leak as yet ;
At last they did get at it really, but
  Still their salvation was an even bet :
The water rush'd through in a way quite puzzling,
While they thrust sheets, shirts, jackets, bales of muslin,

Into the opening ; but all such ingredients
  Would have been vain, and they must have gone
Despite of all their efforts and expedients,   [down,
  But for the pumps : I'm glad to make them known
To all the brother tars who may have need hence,
  For fifty tons of water were upthrown
By them per hour, and they all had been undone,
But for the maker, Mr. Mann, of London.

As day advanced the weather seem'd to abate,
  And then the leak they reckon'd to reduce,
And keep the ship afloat, though three feet yet
  Kept two hand and one chain-pump still in use.
The wind blew fresh again : as it grew late
  A squall came on, and while some guns broke loose,
A gust—which all descriptive power transcends—
Laid with one blast the ship on her beam ends.

There she lay, motionless, and seem'd upset ;
  The water left the hold, and wash'd the decks,
And made a scene men do not soon forget ;
  For they remember battles, fires, and wrecks,
Or any other thing that brings regret,
  Or breaks their hopes, or hearts, or heads, or necks;
Thus drownings are much talk'd of by the divers,
And swimmers, who may chance to be survivors.

Immediately the masts were cut away,
  Both main and mizen : first the mizen went,
The main-mast follow'd ; but the ship still lay
  Like a mere log, and baffled our intent.
Foremast and bowsprit were cut down, and they
  Eased her at last (although we never meant
To part with all till every hope was blighted),
And then with violence the old ship righted.

It may be easily supposed, while this
  Was going on, some people were unquiet,
That passengers would find it much amiss
  To lose their lives, as well as spoil their diet ;
That even the able seaman, deeming his
  Days nearly o'er, might be disposed to riot,
As upon such occasions tars will ask
For grog, and sometimes drink rum from the cask.

There's nought, no doubt, so much the spirit calms
  As rum and true religion : thus it was,
Some plunder'd, some drank spirits, some sung psalms,
  The high wind made the treble, and as bass
The hoarse harsh waves kept time ; fright cured the
  Of all the luckless landsmen's sea-sick maws : [qualms
Strange sounds of wailing, blasphemy, devotion,
Clamour'd in chorus to the roaring ocean.

Perhaps more mischief had been done, but for
   Our Juan, who, with sense beyond his years,
Got to the spirit-room, and stood before
   It with a pair of pistols; and their fears,
As if Death were more dreadful by his door
   Of fire than water, spite of oaths and tears,
Kept still aloof the crew, who, ere they sunk,
Thought it would be becoming to die drunk.

" Give us more grog," they cried, "for it will be
   All one an hour hence." Juan answer'd, " No !
'Tis true that death awaits both you and me,
   But let us die like men, not sink below
Like brutes : "—and thus his dangerous post kept he,
   And none liked to anticipate the blow;
And even Pedrillo, his most reverend tutor,
Was for some rum a disappointed suitor.

The good old gentleman was quite aghast,
   And made a loud and pious lamentation ;
Repented all his sins, and made a last
   Irrevocable vow of reformation ;
Nothing should tempt him more (this peril past)
   To quit his academic occupation,
In cloisters of the classic Salamanca,
To follow Juan's wake, like Sancho Panca.

But now there came a flash of hope once more;
    Day broke, and the wind lull'd: the masts were gone;
The leak increased; shoals round her, but no shore,
    The vessel swam, yet still she held her own.
They tried the pumps again, and though before
    Their desperate efforts seem'd all useless grown,
A glimpse of sunshine set some hands to bale—
The stronger pump'd, the weaker thrumm'd a sail.

Under the vessel's keel the sail was pass'd,
    And for the moment it had some effect;
But with a leak, and not a stick of mast,
    Nor rag of canvas, what could they expect?
But still 'tis best to struggle to the last,
    'Tis never too late to be wholly wreck'd:
. And though 'tis true that man can only die once,
'Tis not so pleasant in the Gulf of Lyons.

There winds and waves had hurl'd them, and from
    Without their will, they carried them away; [thence,
For they were forced with steering to dispense,
    And never had as yet a quiet day
On which they might repose, or even commence
    A jurymast or rudder, or could say
The ship would swim an hour, which, by good luck,
Still swam—though not exactly like a duck.

The wind, in fact, perhaps, was rather less,
  But the ship labour'd so, they scarce could hope
To weather out much longer; the distress
  Was also great with which they had to cope
For want of water, and their solid mess
  Was scant enough: in vain the telescope
Was used—nor sail nor shore appear'd in sight,
Nought but the heavy sea, and coming night.

Again the weather threaten'd,—again blew
  . A gale, and in the fore and after hold
Water appear'd; yet, though the people knew
  All this, the most were patient, and some bold,
Until the chains and leathers were worn through
  Of all our pumps:—a wreck complete she roll'd,
At mercy of the waves, whose mercies are
Like human beings during civil war.

Then came the carpenter, at last, with tears
  In his rough eyes, and told the captain, he
Could do no more: he was a man in years,
  And long had voyaged through many a stormy sea,
And if he wept at length, they were not fears
  That made his eyelids as a woman's be,
But he, poor fellow, had a wife and children,
Two things for dying people quite bewildering.

The ship was evidently settling now
    Fast by the head ; and, all distinction gone,
Some went to prayers again, and made a vow
    Of candles to their saints—but there were none
To pay them with ; and some look'd o'er the bow ;
    Some hoisted out the boats ; and there was one
That begg'd Pedrillo for an absolution,
Who told him to be damn'd—in his confusion.

Some lash'd them in their hammocks ; some put on
    Their best clothes, as if going to a fair ;
Some cursed the day on which they saw the sun,
    And gnash'd their teeth, and howling, tore their hair ;
And others went on as they had begun,
    Getting the boats out, being well aware
That a tight boat will live in a rough sea,
Unless with breakers close beneath her lee.

The worst of all·was, that in their condition,
    Having been several days in great distress,
'Twas difficult to get out such provision
    As now might render their long suffering less :
Men, even when dying, dislike inanition ;
    Their stock was damaged by the weather's stress :
Two casks of biscuit, and a keg of butter,
Were all that could be thrown into the cutter.

K

But in the long-boat they contrived to stow
  Some pounds of bread, though injured by the wet ;
Water, a twenty-gallon cask or so ;
  Six flasks of wine : and they contrived to get
A portion of their beef up from below,
  And with a piece of pork, moreover, met,
But scarce enough to serve them for a luncheon—
Then there was rum, eight gallons in a puncheon.

The other boats, the yawl and pinnace, had
  Been stove in the beginning of the gale ;
And the long-boat's condition was but bad,
  As there were but two blankets for a sail,
And one oar for a mast, which a young lad
  Threw in by good luck over the ship's rail ;
And two boats could not hold, far less be stored,
To save one half the people then on board.

'Twas twilight, and the sunless day went down
  Over the waste of waters ; like a veil,
Which, if withdrawn, would but disclose the frown
  Of one whose hate is mask'd but to assail.
Thus to their hopeless eyes the night was shown,
  And grimly darkled o'er the faces pale,
And the dim desolate deep : twelve days had Fear
Been their familiar, and now Death was here.

Some trial had been making at a raft,
 With little hope in such a rolling sea,
A sort of thing at which one would have laugh'd,
 If any laughter at such times could be,
Unless with people who too much have quaff'd,
 And have a kind of wild and horrid glee,
Half epileptical, and half hysterical :—
Their preservation would have been a miracle.

At half-past eight o'clock, booms, hencoops, spars,
 And all things, for a chance, had been cast loose
That still could keep afloat the struggling tars,
 For yet they strove, although of no great use :
There was no light in heaven but a few stars,
 The boats put off o'ercrowded with their crews;
She gave a heel, and then a lurch to port,
And, going down head foremost—sunk, in short.

Then rose from sea to sky the wild farewell—
 Then shriek'd the timid, and stood still the brave—
Then some leap'd overboard with dreadful yell,
 As eager to anticipate their grave ;
And the sea yawn'd around her like a hell,
 And down she suck'd with her the whirling wave,
Like one who grapples with his enemy,
And strives to strangle him before he die.

K 2

And first one universal shriek there rush'd,
  Louder than the loud ocean, like a crash
Of echoing thunder ; and then all was hush'd,
  Save the wild wind and the remorseless dash
Of billows; but at intervals there gush'd,
  Accompanied with a convulsive splash,
A solitary shriek, the bubbling cry
Of some strong swimmer in his agony.

The boats, as stated, had got off before,
  And in them crowded several of the crew ;
And yet their present hope was hardly more
  Than what it had been, for so strong it blew
There was slight chance of reaching any shore ;
  And then they were too many, though so few—
Nine in the cutter, thirty in the boat,
Were counted in them when they got afloat.

All the rest perish'd ; near two hundred souls
  Had left their bodies ; and, what's worse, alas!
When over Catholics the ocean rolls,
  They must wait several weeks before a mass
Takes off one peck of purgatorial coals,
  Because, till people know what's come to pass,
They won't lay out their money on the dead—
It costs three francs for every mass that's said.

Juan got into the long-boat, and there
    Contrived to help Pedrillo to a place ;
It seem'd as if they had exchanged their care,
    For Juan wore the magisterial face
Which courage gives, while poor Pedrillo's pair
    Of eyes were crying for their owner's case :
Battista, though (a name call'd shortly Tita),
Was lost by getting at some aqua-vita.

Pedro, his valet, too, he tried to save,
    But the same cause, conducive to his loss,
Left him so drunk, he jump'd into the wave,
    As o'er the cutter's edge he tried to cross,
And so he found a wine-and-watery grave ;
    They could not rescue him although so close,
Because the sea ran higher every minute,
And for the boat—the crew kept crowding in it.

A small old spaniel—which had been Don Jóse's,
    His father's, whom he loved, as ye may think,
For on such things the memory reposes
    With tenderness—stood howling on the brink,
Knowing, (dogs have such intellectual noses !)
    No doubt, the vessel was about to sink ;
And Juan caught him up, and ere he stepp'd
Off threw him in, then after him he leap'd.

He also stuff'd his money where he could
　About his person, and Pedrillo's too,
Who let him do, in fact, whate'er he would,
　Not knowing what himself to say, or do,
As every rising wave his dread renew'd ;
　But Juan, trusting they might still get through,
And deeming there were remedies for any ill,
Thus re-embark'd his tutor and his spaniel.

'Twas a rough night, and blew so stiffly yet,
　That the sail was becalm'd between the seas,
Though on the wave's high top too much to set,
　They dared not take it in for all the breeze :
Each sea curl'd o'er the stern, and kept them wet,
　And made them bale without a moment's ease,
So that themselves as well as hopes were damp'd,
And the poor little cutter quickly swamp'd.

Nine souls more went in her : the long-boat still
　Kept above water, with an oar for mast,
Two blankets stitch'd together, answering ill
　Instead of sail, were to the oar made fast :
Though every wave roll'd menacing to fill,
　And present peril all before surpass'd,
They grieved for those who perish'd with the cutter,
And also for the biscuit-casks and butter.

The sun rose red and fiery, a sure sign
  Of the continuance of the gale : to run
Before the sea until it should grow fine,
  Was all that for the present could be done :
A few tea-spoonfuls of their rum and wine
  Were served out to the people, who begun
To faint, and damaged bread wet through the bags,
And most of them had little clothes but rags.

They counted thirty, crowded in a space
  Which left scarce room for motion or exertion ;
They did their best to modify their case,
  One half sate up, though numb'd with the immersion,
While t'other half were laid down in their place,
  At watch and watch ; thus, shivering like the tertian
Ague in its cold fit, they fill'd their boat,
With nothing but the sky for a great coat.

'Tis very certain the desire of life
  Prolongs it : this is obvious to physicians,
When patients, neither plagued with friends nor wife,
  Survive through very desperate conditions,
Because they still can hope, nor shines the knife
  Nor shears of Atropos before their visions :
Despair of all recovery spoils longevity,
And makes men's miseries of alarming brevity.

'Tis said that persons living on annuities
  Are longer lived than others,—God knows why,
Unless to plague the grantors,—yet so true it is,
  That some, I really think, *do* never die ;
Of any creditors the worst a Jew it is,
  And *that*'s their mode of furnishing supply :
In my young days they lent me cash that way,
Which I found very troublesome to pay.

'Tis thus with people in an open boat,
  They live upon the love of life, and bear
More than can be believed, or even thought,
  And stand like rocks the tempest's wear and tear ;
And hardship still has been the sailor's lot,
  Since Noah's ark went cruising here and there ;
She had a curious crew as well as cargo,
Like the first old Greek privateer, the Argo.

But man is a carnivorous production,
  And must have meals, at least one meal a day ;
He cannot live, like woodcocks, upon suction,
  But, like the shark and tiger, must have prey ;
Although his anatomical construction
  Bears vegetables, in a grumbling way,
Your labouring people think beyond all question
Beef, veal, and mutton, better for digestion.

And thus it was with this our hapless crew ;
  For on the third day there came on a calm,
And though at first their strength it might renew,
  And lying on their weariness like balm,
Lull'd them like turtles sleeping on the blue
  Of ocean, when they woke they felt a qualm,
And fell all ravenously on their provision,
Instead of hoarding it with due precision.

The consequence was easily foreseen—
  They ate up all they had, and drank their wine,
In spite of all remonstrances, and then
  On what, in fact, next day were they to dine ?
They hoped the wind would rise, these foolish men !
  And carry them to shore ; these hopes were fine,
But as they had but one oar, and that brittle,
It would have been more wise to save their victual.

The fourth day came, but not a breath of air,
  And Ocean slumber'd like an unwean'd child :
The fifth day, and their boat lay floating there,
  The sea and sky were blue, and clear, and mild—
With their one oar (I wish they had had a pair)
  What could they do ? and hunger's rage grew wild:
So Juan's spaniel, spite of his entreating,
Was kill'd, and portion'd out for present eating.

On the sixth day they fed upon his hide,
    And Juan, who had still refused, because
The creature was his father's dog that died,
    Now feeling all the vulture in his jaws,
With some remorse received (though first denied)
    As a great favour one of the fore-paws,
Which he divided with Pedrillo, who
Devour'd it, longing for the other too.

The seventh day, and no wind—the burning sun
    Blister'd and scorch'd, and, stagnant on the sea,
They lay like carcasses ; and hope was none,
    Save in the breeze that came not : savagely
They glared upon each other—all was done,
    Water, and wine, and food,—and you might see
The longings of the cannibal arise
(Although they spoke not) in their wolfish eyes.

At length one whisper'd his companion, who
    Whisper'd another, and thus it went round,
And then into a hoarser murmur grew,
    An ominous, and wild, and desperate sound ;
And when his comrade's thought each sufferer knew,
    'Twas but his own, suppress'd till now, he found :
And out they spoke of lots for flesh and blood,
And who should die to be his fellow's food.

But ere they came to this, they that day shared
  Some leathern caps, and what remain'd of shoes;
And then they look'd around them, and despair'd,
  And none to be the sacrifice would choose;
At length the lots were torn up, and prepared,
  But of materials that must shock the Muse—
Having no paper, for the want of better,
They took by force from Juan Julia's letter.

Then lots were made, and mark'd, and mix'd, and
  In silent horror, and their distribution   [handed
Lull'd even the savage hunger which demanded,
  Like the Promethean vulture, this pollution;
None in particular had sought or plann'd it,
  'Twas nature gnaw'd them to this resolution,
By which none were permitted to be neuter—
And the lot fell on Juan's luckless tutor.

He but requested to be bled to death :
  The surgeon had his instruments, and bled
Pedrillo, and so gently ebb'd his breath,
  You hardly could perceive when he was dead.
He died as born, a Catholic in faith,
  Like most in the belief in which they're bred,
And first a little crucifix he kiss'd,
And then held out his jugular and wrist.

The surgeon, as there was no other fee,
    Had his first choice of morsels for his pains ;
But being thirstiest at the moment, he
    Preferr'd a draught from the fast-flowing veins :
Part was divided, part thrown in the sea,
    And such things as the entrails and the brains
Regaled two sharks, who follow'd o'er the billow—
The sailors ate the rest of poor Pedrillo.

The sailors ate him, all save three or four,
    Who were not quite so fond of animal food ;
To these was added Juan, who, before
    Refusing his own spaniel, hardly could
Feel now his appetite increased much more ;
    'Twas not to be expected that he should,
Even in extremity of their disaster,
Dine with them on his pastor and his master.

'Twas better that he did not ; for, in fact,
    The consequence was awful in the extreme ;
For they, who were most ravenous in the act,
    Went raging mad—Lord! how they did blaspheme!
And foam, and roll, with strange convulsions rack'd,
    Drinking salt-water like a mountain-stream ;
Tearing, and grinning, howling, screeching, swearing,
And, with hyæna-laughter, died despairing.

Their numbers were much thinn'd by this infliction,
　　And all the rest were thin enough, Heaven knows ;
And some of them had lost their recollection,
　　Happier than they who still perceived their woes ;
But others ponder'd on a new dissection,
　　As if not warn'd sufficiently by those
Who had already perish'd, suffering madly,
For having used their appetites so sadly.

And next they thought upon the master's mate,
　　As fattest ; but he saved himself, because,
Besides being much averse from such a fate,
　　There were some other reasons : the first was,
He had been rather indisposed of late ;
　　And that which chiefly proved his saving clause,
Was a small present made to him at Cadiz,
By general subscription of the ladies.

Of poor Pedrillo something still remain'd,
　　But was used sparingly,—some were afraid,
And others still their appetites constrain'd,
　　Or but at times a little supper made ;
All except Juan, who throughout abstain'd,
　　Chewing a piece of bamboo, and some lead :
At length they caught two boobies, and a noddy,
And then they left off eating the dead body.

And if Pedrillo's fate should shocking be,
  Remember Ugolino condescends
To eat the head of his arch-enemy
  The moment after he politely ends
His tale : if foes be food in hell, at sea
  'Tis surely fair to dine upon our friends,
When shipwreck's short allowance grows too scanty,
Without being much more horrible than Dante.

And the same night there fell a shower of rain,
  For which their mouths gaped, like the cracks of earth
When dried to summer dust ; till taught by pain,
  Men really know not what good water's worth ;
If you had been in Turkey or in Spain,
  Or with a famish'd boat's-crew had your berth,
Or in the desert heard the camel's bell,
You'd wish yourself where Truth is—in a well.

It pour'd down torrents, but they were no richer,
  Until they found a ragged piece of sheet,
Which served them as a sort of spongy pitcher,
  And when they deem'd its moisture was complete,
They wrung it out, and though a thirsty ditcher
  Might not have thought the scanty draught so sweet
As a full pot of porter, to their thinking
They ne'er till now had known the joys of drinking.

And their baked lips, with many a bloody crack,
  Suck'd in the moisture, which like nectar stream'd ;
Their throats were ovens, their swoln tongues were black
  As the rich man's in hell, who vainly scream'd
To beg the beggar, who could not rain back
  A drop of dew, when every drop had seem'd
To taste of heaven—If this be true, indeed,
  Some Christians have a comfortable creed.

There were two fathers in this ghastly crew,
  And with them their two sons, of whom the one
Was more robust and hardy to the view,
  But he died early ; and when he was gone,
His nearest messmate told his sire, who threw
  One glance at him, and said, " Heaven's will be done !
I can do nothing," and he saw him thrown
Into the deep without a tear or groan.

The other father had a weaklier child,
  Of a soft cheek, and aspect delicate ;
But the boy bore up long, and with a mild
  And patient spirit held aloof his fate ;
Little he said, and now and then he smiled,
  As if to win a part from off the weight
He saw increasing on his father's heart,
With the deep deadly thought, that they must part.

And o'er him bent his sire, and never raised
　His eyes from off his face, but wiped the foam
From his pale lips, and ever on him gazed,
　And when the wish'd-for shower at length was come,
And the boy's eyes, which the dull film half glazed,
　Brighten'd, and for a moment seem'd to roam,
He squeezed from out a rag some drops of rain
Into his dying child's mouth—but in vain.

The boy expired—the father held the clay,
　And look'd upon it long, and when at last
Death left no doubt, and the dead burthen lay
　Stiff on his heart, and pulse and hope were past,
He watch'd it wistfully, until away
　'Twas borne by the rude wave wherein 'twas cast;
Then he himself sunk down all dumb and shivering,
And gave no sign of life, save his limbs quivering.

Now overhead a rainbow, bursting through
　The scattering clouds, shone, spanning the dark sea,
Resting its bright base on the quivering blue;
　And all within its arch appear'd to be
Clearer than that without, and its wide hue
　Wax'd broad and waving, like a banner free,
Then changed like to a bow that's bent, and then
Forsook the dim eyes of these shipwreck'd men.

It changed, of course ; a heavenly chameleon,
  The airy child of vapour and the sun,
Brought forth in purple, cradled in vermilion,
  Baptized in molten gold, and swathed in dun,
Glittering like crescents o'er a Turk's pavilion,
  And blending every colour into one,
Just like a black eye in a recent scuffle
(For sometimes we must box without the muffle).

Our shipwreck'd seamen thought it a good omen—
  It is as well to think so, now and then ;
'Twas an old custom of the Greek and Roman,
  And may become of great advantage when
Folks are discouraged ; and most surely no men
  Had greater need to nerve themselves again
Than these, and so this rainbow look'd like hope—
Quite a celestial kaleidoscope.

About this time a beautiful white bird,
  Web-footed, not unlike a dove in size
And plumage (probably it might have err'd
  Upon its course), pass'd oft before their eyes,
And tried to perch, although it saw and heard
  The men within the boat, and in this guise
It came and went, and flutter'd round them till
Night fell :—this seem'd a better omen still.

L

But in this case I also must remark,
  'Twas well this bird of promise did not perch,
Because the tackle of our shatter'd bark
  Was not so safe for roosting as a church;
And had it been the dove from Noah's ark,
  Returning there from her successful search,
Which in their way that moment chanced to fall,
They would have eat her, olive-branch and all.

With twilight it again came on to blow,
  But not with violence; the stars shone out,
The boat made way; yet now they were so low,
  They knew not where nor what they were about;
Some fancied they saw land, and some said "No!"
  The frequent fog-banks gave them cause to doubt—
Some swore that they heard breakers, others guns,
And all mistook about the latter once.

As morning broke, the light wind died away,
  When he who had the watch sung out and swore,
If 'twas not land that rose with the sun's ray,
  He wish'd that land he never might see more:
And the rest rubb'd their eyes, and saw a bay, [shore;
  Or thought they saw, and shaped their course for
For shore it was, and gradually grew
Distinct, and high, and palpable to view.

And then of these some part burst into tears,
  And others, looking with a stupid stare,
Could not yet separate their hopes from fears,
  And seem'd as if they had no further care ;
While a few pray'd—(the first time for some years)—
  And at the bottom of the boat three were
Asleep : they shook them by the hand and head,
And tried to awaken them, but found them dead.

The day before, fast sleeping on the water,
  They found a turtle of the hawk's-bill kind,
And by good fortune, gliding softly, caught her,
  Which yielded a day's life, and to their mind
Proved even still a more nutritious matter,
  Because it left encouragement behind :
They·thought that in such perils, more than chance
Had sent them this for their deliverance.

The land appear'd a high and rocky coast,
  And higher grew the mountains as they drew,
Set by a current, toward it : they were lost
  In various conjectures, for none knew
To what part of the earth they had been tost,
  So changeable had been the winds that blew ;
Some thought it was Mount Ætna, some the highlands
Of Candia, Cyprus, Rhodes, or other islands.

Meantime the current, with a rising gale,
    Still set them onwards to the welcome shore,
Like Charon's bark of spectres, dull and pale :
    Their living freight was now reduced to four,
And three dead, whom their strength could not avail
    To heave into the deep with those before,
Though the two sharks still follow'd them, and dash'd
The spray into their faces as they splash'd.

Famine, despair, cold, thirst, and heat, had done
    Their work on them by turns, and thinn'd them to
Such things a mother had not known her son
    Amidst the skeletons of that gaunt crew ;
By night chill'd, by day scorch'd, thus one by one
    They perish'd, until wither'd to these few,
But chiefly by a species of self-slaughter,
In washing down Pedrillo with salt water.

As they drew nigh the land, which now was seen
    Unequal in its aspect here and there,
They felt the freshness of its growing green,
    That waved in forest-tops, and smooth'd the air,
And fell upon their glazed eyes like a screen
    From glistening waves, and skies so hot and bare—
Lovely seem'd any object that should sweep
Away the vast, salt, dread, eternal deep.

The shore look'd wild, without a trace of man,
   And girt by formidable waves; but they
Were mad for land, and thus their course they ran,
   Though right ahead the roaring breakers lay:
A reef between them also now began
   To show its boiling surf and bounding spray,
But finding no place for their landing better,
They ran the boat for shore,—and overset her.

But in his native stream, the Guadalquivir,
   Juan to lave his youthful limbs was wont;
And having learnt to swim in that sweet river,
   Had often turn'd the art to some account:
A better swimmer you could scarce see ever,
   He could, perhaps, have pass'd the Hellespont,
As once (a feat on which ourselves we prided)
Leander, Mr. Ekenhead, and I did.

So here, though faint, emaciated, and stark,
   He buoy'd his boyish limbs, and strove to ply
With the quick wave, and gain, ere it was dark,
   The beach which lay before him, high and dry:
The greatest danger here was from a shark,
   That carried off his neighbour by the thigh;
As for the other two, they could not swim,
So nobody arrived on shore but him.

Nor yet had he arrived but for the oar,
    Which, providentially for him, was wash'd
Just as his feeble arms could strike no more,
    And the hard wave o'erwhelm'd him as 'twas dash'd
Within his grasp; he clung to it, and sore
    The waters beat while he thereto was lash'd;
At last, with swimming, wading, scrambling, he
Roll'd on the beach, half senseless, from the sea:

There, breathless, with his digging nails he clung
    Fast to the sand, lest the returning wave,
From whose reluctant roar his life he wrung,
    Should suck him back to her insatiate grave:
And there he lay, full length, where he was flung,
    Before the entrance of a cliff-worn cave,
With just enough of life to feel its pain,
And deem that it was saved, perhaps in vain.

With slow and staggering effort he arose,
    But sunk again upon his bleeding knee
And quivering hand; and then he look'd for those
    Who long had been his mates upon the sea;
But none of them appear'd to share his woes,
    Save one, a corpse, from out the famish'd three,
Who died two days before, and now had found
An unknown barren beach for burial-ground.

And as he gazed, his dizzy brain spun fast,
   And down he sunk ; and as he sunk, the sand
Swam round and round, and all his senses pass'd.
   He fell upon his side, and his stretch'd hand
Droop'd dripping on the oar (their jury-mast),
   And, like a wither'd lily, on the land
His slender frame and pallid aspect lay,
As fair a thing as e'er was form'd of clay.

How long in his damp trance young Juan lay
   He knew not, for the earth was gone for him,
And time had nothing more of night nor day
   For his congealing blood, and senses dim ;
And how this heavy faintness pass'd away
   He knew not, till each painful pulse and limb,
And tingling vein, seem'd throbbing back to life,
For Death, though vanquish'd, still retired with strife.

From THE SAME.—CANTO II.

IT was the cooling hour, just when the rounded
   Red sun sinks down behind the azure hill,
Which then seems as if the whole earth it bounded,
   Circling all nature, hush'd, and dim, and still,
With the far mountain-crescent half surrounded
   On one side, and the deep sea calm and chill,
Upon the other, and the rosy sky,
With one star sparkling through it like an eye.

And thus they wander'd forth, and hand in hand,
　Over the shining pebbles and the shells,
Glided along the smooth and harden'd sand,
　And in the worn and wild receptacles
Work'd by the storms, yet work'd as it were plann'd,
　In hollow halls, with sparry roofs and cells,
They turn'd to rest; and, each clasp'd by an arm,
Yielded to the deep twilight's purple charm.

They look'd up to the sky, whose floating glow
　Spread like a rosy ocean, vast and bright;
They gazed upon the glittering sea below,
　Whence the broad moon rose circling into sight;
They heard the waves' splash, and the wind so low,
　And saw each other's dark eyes darting light
Into each other—and, beholding this,
Their lips drew near, and clung into a kiss;

A long, long kiss, a kiss of youth, and love,
　And beauty, all concentrating like rays
Into one focus, kindled from above;
　Such kisses as belong to early days,
Where heart, and soul, and sense, in concert move,
　And the blood's lava, and the pulse a blaze,
Each kiss a heart-quake,—for a kiss's strength,
I think it must be reckon'd by its length.

By length I mean duration ; theirs endured [reckon'd ;
Heaven knows how long—no doubt they never
And if they had, they could not have secured
The sum of their sensations to a second :
They had not spoken ; but they felt allured,
As if their souls and lips each other beckon'd,
Which, being join'd, like swarming bees they clung—
Their hearts the flowers from whence the honey sprung.

They were alone, but not alone as they
Who shut in chambers think it loneliness ;
The silent ocean, and the starlight bay,
The twilight glow, which momently grew less,
The voiceless sands, and dropping caves, that lay
Around them, made them to each other press,
As if there were no life beneath the sky
Save theirs, and that their life could never die.

They fear'd no eyes nor ears on that lone beach,
They felt no terrors from the night ; they were
All in all to each other ; though their speech
Was broken words, they *thought* a language there,—
And all the burning tongues the passions teach
Found in one sigh the best interpreter
Of nature's oracle—first love,—that all
Which Eve has left her daughters since her fall.

Haidée spoke not of scruples, ask'd no vows,
  Nor offer'd any ; she had never heard
Of plight and promises to be a spouse,
  Or perils by a loving maid incurr'd ;
She was all which pure ignorance allows,
  And flew to her young mate like a young bird,
And never having dreamt of falsehood, she
Had not one word to say of constancy.

She loved, and was beloved—she adored,
  And she was worshipp'd ; after nature's fashion,
Their intense souls, into each other pour'd,
  If souls could die, had perish'd in that passion,—
But by degrees their senses were restored,
  Again to be o'ercome, again to dash on ;
And, beating 'gainst *his* bosom, Haidée's heart
Felt as if never more to beat apart.

Alas ! they were so young, so beautiful,
  So lonely, loving, helpless, and the hour
Was that in which the heart is always full,
  And, having o'er itself no further power,
Prompts deeds eternity cannot annul,
  But pays off moments in an endless shower
Of hell-fire—all prepared for people giving
Pleasure or pain to one another living.

Alas! for Juan and Haidée! they were
　So loving and so lovely—till then never,
Excepting our first parents, such a pair
　Had run the risk of being damn'd for ever;
And Haidée, being devout as well as fair,
　Had, doubtless, heard about the Stygian river,
And hell and purgatory—but forgot
Just in the very crisis she should not.

They look upon each other, and their eyes
　Gleam in the moonlight; and her white arm clasps
Round Juan's head, and his around her lies
　Half buried in the tresses which it grasps;
She sits upon his knee, and drinks his sighs,
　He hers, until they end in broken gasps;
And thus they form a group that's quite antique,
Half naked, loving, natural, and Greek.

And when those deep and burning moments pass'd,
　And Juan sunk to sleep within her arms,
She slept not, but all tenderly, though fast,
　Sustain'd his head upon her bosom's charms;
And now and then her eye to heaven is cast,
　And then on the pale cheek her breast now warms,
Pillow'd on her o'erflowing heart, which pants
With all it granted, and with all it grants.

An infant when it gazes on a light,
    A child the moment when it drains the breast,
A devotee when soars the Host in sight,
    An Arab with a stranger for a guest,
A sailor when the prize has struck in fight,
    A miser filling his most hoarded chest,
Feel rapture ; but not such true joy are reaping
As they who watch o'er what they love while sleeping.

For there it lies so tranquil, so beloved,
    All that it hath of life with us is living ;
So gentle, stirless, helpless, and unmoved,
    And all unconscious of the joy 'tis giving ;
All it hath felt, inflicted, pass'd, and proved,
    Hush'd into depths beyond the watcher's diving ;
There lies the thing we love with all its errors
And all its charms, like death without its terrors.

The lady watch'd her lover—and that hour
    Of Love's, and Night's, and Ocean's solitude,
O'erflow'd her soul with their united power ;
    Amidst the barren sand and rocks so rude
She and her wave-worn love had made their bower,
    Where nought upon their passion could intrude,
And all the stars that crowded the blue space
Saw nothing happier than her glowing face.

Alas! the love of women! it is known
　To be a lovely and a fearful thing;
For all of theirs upon that die is thrown,
　And if 'tis lost, life hath no more to bring
To them but mockeries of the past alone,
　And their revenge is as the tiger's spring,
Deadly, and quick, and crushing; yet, as real
Torture is theirs, what they inflict they feel.

They are right; for man, to man so oft unjust,
　Is always so to women; one sole bond
Awaits them, treachery is all their trust;
　Taught to conceal, their bursting hearts despond
Over their idol, till some wealthier lust
　Buys them in marriage—and what rests beyond?
A thankless husband, next a faithless lover,
Then dressing, nursing, praying, and all's over.

Some take a lover, some take drams or prayeis,
　Some mind their household, others dissipation,
Some run away, and but exchange their cares,
　Losing the advantage of a virtuous station;
Few changes e'er can better their affairs,
　Theirs being an unnatural situation,
From the dull palace to the dirty hovel:
Some play the devil, and then write a novel.

Haidée was Nature's bride, and knew not this:
　　Haidée was Passion's child, born where the sun
Showers triple light, and scorches even the kiss
　　Of his gazelle-eyed daughters ; she was one
Made but to love, to feel that she was his
　　Who was her chosen : what was said or done
Elsewhere was nothing.　She had nought to fear,
Hope, care, nor love beyond,—her heart beat *here*.

And oh ! that quickening of the heart, that beat !
　　How much it costs us ! yet each rising throb
Is in its cause as its effect so sweet,
　　That Wisdom, ever on the watch to rob
Joy of its alchemy, and to repeat
　　Fine truths ; even Conscience, too, has a tough job
To make us understand each good old maxim,
So good—I wonder Castlereagh don't tax 'em.

And now 'twas done—on the lone shore were plighted
　　Their hearts ; the stars, their nuptial torches, shed
Beauty upon the beautiful they lighted :　.
　　Ocean their witness, and the cave their bed,
By their own feelings hallow'd and united,
　　Their priest was Solitude, and they were wed :
And they were happy, for to their young eyes
Each was an angel, and earth paradise.

From THE SAME.—CANTO III.

AND further on a group of Grecian girls,
  The first and tallest her white kerchief waving,
Were strung together like a row of pearls,
  Link'd hand in hand, and dancing : each too having
Down her white neck long floating auburn curls—
  (The least of which would set ten poets raving) ;
Their leader sang—and bounded to her song,
With choral step and voice, the virgin throng.

And here, assembled cross-legg'd round their trays,
  Small social parties just begun to dine ;
Pilaus and meats of all sorts met the gaze,
  And flasks of Samian and of Chian wine,
And sherbet cooling in the porous vase ;
  Above them their dessert grew on its vine,
The orange and pomegranate nodding o'er
Dropp'd in their laps, scarce pluck'd, their mellow store.

A band of children, round a snow-white ram,
  There wreathe his venerable horns with flowers ;
While peaceful as if still an unwean'd lamb,
  The patriarch of the flock all gently cowers
His sober head, majestically tame,
  Or eats from out the palm, or playful lowers
His brow, as if in act to butt, and then
Yielding to their small hands, draws back again.

Their classical profiles, and glittering dresses,
   Their large black eyes, and soft seraphic cheeks,
Crimson as cleft pomegranates, their long tresses,
   The gesture which enchants, the eye that speaks,
The innocence which happy childhood blesses,
   Made quite a picture of these little Greeks;
So that the philosophical beholder
Sigh'd for their sakes—that they should e'er grow older.

From THE SAME.—CANTO III.

OF all the dresses I select Haidée's:
   She wore two jelicks—one was of pale yellow;
Of azure, pink, and white was her chemise—
   'Neath which her breast heaved like a little billow;
With buttons form'd of pearls as large as peas,
   All gold and crimson shone her jelick's fellow,
And the striped white gauze baracan that bound her,
Like fleecy clouds about the moon, flow'd round her.

One large gold bracelet clasp'd each lovely arm,
   Lockless—so pliable from the pure gold
That the hand stretch'd and shut it without harm,
   The limb which it adorn'd its only mould;
So beautiful—its very shape would charm,
   And clinging as if loath to lose its hold,
The purest ore enclosed the whitest skin
That e'er by precious metal was held in.

Around, as princess of her father's land,
  A like gold bar above her instep roll'd
Announced her rank ; twelve rings were on her hand ;
  Her hair was starr'd with gems ; her veil's fine fold
Below her breast was fasten'd with a band
  Of lavish pearls, whose worth could scarce be told ;
Her orange silk full Turkish trousers furl'd
About the prettiest ankle in the world.

Her hair's long auburn waves down to her heel
  Flow'd like an Alpine torrent which the sun
Dyes with his morning light,—and would conceal
  Her person if allow'd at large to run,
And still they seem'd resentfully to feel
  The silken fillet's curb, and sought to shun
Their bonds whene'er some Zephyr caught began
To offer his young pinion as her fan.

Round her she made an atmosphere of life,
  The very air seem'd lighter from her eyes,
They were so soft and beautiful, and rife
  With all we can imagine of the skies,
And pure as Psyche ere she grew a wife—
  Too pure even for the purest human ties ;
Her overpowering presence made you feel
It would not be idolatry to kneel.

M

Her eyelashes, though dark as night, were tinged
   (It is the country's custom), but in vain ;
For those large black eyes were so blackly fringed,
   The glossy rebels mock'd the jetty stain,
And in their native beauty stood avenged :
   Her nails were touch'd with henna; but again
The power of art was turn'd to nothing, for
They could not look more rosy than before.

The henna should be deeply dyed to make
   The skin relieved appear more fairly fair ;
She had no need of this, day ne'er will break
   On mountain-tops more heavenly white than her :
The eye might doubt if it were well awake,
   She was so like a vision ; I might err,
But Shakspeare also says, 'tis very silly
" To gild refined gold, or paint the lily."

Juan had on a shawl of black and gold,
   But a white baracan, and so transparent
The sparkling gems beneath you might behold,
   Like small stars through the milky way apparent ;
His turban furl'd in many a graceful fold,
   An emerald aigrette with Haidée's hair in 't
Surmounted, as its clasp, a glowing crescent,
Whose rays shone ever trembling, but incessant.

From THE SAME.—CANTO III.

THE isles of Greece, the isles of Greece !
  Where burning Sappho loved and sung,
Where grew the arts of war and peace,
  Where Delos rose, and Phœbus sprung !
Eternal summer gilds them yet,
But all, except their sun, is set.

The Scian and the Teian muse,
  The hero's harp, the lover's lute,
Have found the fame your shores refuse :
  Their place of birth alone is mute
To sounds which echo further west
Than your sires' " Islands of the Blest."

The mountains look on Marathon—
  And Marathon looks on the sea ;
And musing there an hour alone,
  I dream'd that Greece might still be free ;
For standing on the Persians' grave,
I could not deem myself a slave.

A king sate on the rocky brow
  Which looks o'er sea-born Salamis ;
And ships, by thousands, lay below,
  And men in nations ;—all were his !

M 2

He counted them at break of day—
And when the sun set where were they?

And where are they? and where art thou,
　My country? On thy voiceless shore
The heroic lay is tuneless now—
　The heroic bosom beats no more!
And must thy lyre, so long divine,
Degenerate into hands like mine?

'Tis something, in the dearth of fame,
　Though link'd among a fetter'd race,
To feel at least a patriot's shame,
　Even as I sing, suffuse my face;
For what is left the poet here?
For Greeks a blush—for Greece a tear.

Must *we* but weep o'er days more blest?
　Must *we* but blush?—Our fathers bled.
Earth! render back from out thy breast
　A remnant of our Spartan dead!
Of the three hundred grant but three,
To make a new Thermopylæ!

What, silent still? and silent all?
　Ah! no;—the voices of the dead

Sound like a distant torrent's fall,
  And answer, " Let one living head,
But one arise,—we come, we come ! "
'Tis but the living who are dumb.

In vain—in vain : strike other chords ;
  Fill high the cup with Samian wine !
Leave battles to the Turkish hordes,
  And shed the blood of Scio's vine !
Hark ! rising to the ignoble call—
How answers each bold Bacchanal !

You have the Pyrrhic dance as yet ;
  Where is the Pyrrhic phalanx gone ?
Of two such lessons, why forget
  The nobler and the manlier one ?
You have the letters Cadmus gave—
Think ye he meant them for a slave ?

Fill high the bowl with Samian wine !
  We will not think of themes like these !
It made Anacreon's song divine :
  He served—but served Polycrates—
A tyrant ; but our masters then
Were still, at least, our countrymen.

The tyrant of the Chersonese
  Was freedom's best and bravest friend;
That tyrant was Miltiades!
  Oh! that the present hour would lend
Another despot of the kind!
Such chains as his were sure to bind.

Fill high the bowl with Samian wine!
  On Suli's rock, and Parga's shore,
Exists the remnant of a line
  Such as the Doric mothers bore;
And there, perhaps, some seed is sown,
The Heracleidan blood might own.

Trust not for freedom to the Franks—
  They have a king who buys and sells;
In native swords, and native ranks,
  The only hope of courage dwells:
But Turkish force, and Latin fraud,
Would break your shield, however broad.

Fill high the bowl with Samian wine!
  Our virgins dance beneath the shade—
I see their glorious black eyes shine;
  But gazing on each glowing maid,
My own the burning tear-drop laves,
To think such breasts must suckle slaves.

Place me on Sunium's marbled steep,
   Where nothing, save the waves and I,
May hear our mutual murmurs sweep;
   There, swan-like, let me sing and die:
A land of slaves shall ne'er be mine—
Dash down yon cup of Samian wine!

From THE SAME.—CANTO III.

T' OUR tale.—The feast was over, the slaves gone,
   The dwarfs and dancing girls had all retired;
The Arab lore and poet's song were done,
   And every sound of revelry expired;
The lady and her lover, left alone,
   The rosy flood of twilight's sky admired;—
Ave Maria! o'er the earth and sea,
That heavenliest hour of Heaven is worthiest thee!

Ave Maria! blessed be the hour!
   The time, the clime, the spot, where I so oft
Have felt that moment in its fullest power
   Sink o'er the earth so beautiful and soft,
While swung the deep bell in the distant tower,
   Or the faint dying day-hymn stole aloft,
And not a breath crept through the rosy air,
And yet the forest leaves seem'd stirr'd with prayer.

Ave Maria ! 'tis the hour of prayer !
　Ave Maria ! 'tis the hour of love !
Ave Maria ! may our spirits dare
　Look up to thine and to thy Son's above !
Ave Maria ! oh that face so fair !
　Those downcast eyes beneath the Almighty dove—
What though 'tis but a pictured image strike,
That painting is no idol,—'tis too like.

Some kinder casuists are pleased to say,
　In nameless print—that I have no devotion ;
But set those persons down with me to pray,
　And you shall see who has the properest notion
Of getting into heaven the shortest way ;
　My altars are the mountains and the ocean,
Earth, air, stars,—all that springs from the great Whole,
Who hath produced, and will receive the soul.

Sweet hour of twilight !—in the solitude
　Of the pine forest, and the silent shore
Which bounds Ravenna's immemorial wood,
　Rooted where once the Adrian wave flow'd o'er,
To where the last Cæsarean fortress stood,
　Evergreen forest ! which Boccaccio's lore
And Dryden's lay made haunted ground to me,
How have I loved the twilight hour and thee !

The shrill cicalas, people of the pine,
    Making their summer lives one ceaseless song,
Were the sole echoes, save my steed's and mine,
    And vesper bell's that rose the boughs along;
The spectre huntsman of Onesti's line,
·   His hell-dogs, and their chase, and the fair throng
Which learn'd from this example not to fly
From a true lover,—shadow'd my mind's eye.

Oh, Hesperus ! thou bringest all good things—
    Home to the weary, to the hungry cheer,
To the young bird the parent's brooding wings,
    The welcome stall to the o'erlabour'd steer;
Whate'er of peace about our hearthstone clings,
    Whate'er our household gods protect of dear,
Are gather'd round us by thy look of rest;
Thou bring'st the child, too, to the mother's breast.

Soft hour ! which wakes the wish and melts the heart
    Of those who sail the seas, on the first day
When they from their sweet friends are torn apart;
    Or fills with love the pilgrim on his way
As the far bell of vesper makes him start,
    Seeming to weep the dying day's decay;
Is this a fancy which our reason scorns ?
Ah ! surely nothing dies but something mourns !

When Nero perish'd by the justest doom
  Which ever the destroyer yet destroy'd,
Amidst the roar of liberated Rome,
  Of nations freed, and the world overjoy'd,
Some hands unseen strew'd flowers upon his tomb :
  Perhaps the weakness of a heart not void   ·
Of feeling for some kindness done, when power
Had left the wretch an uncorrupted hour.

From THE SAME.—CANTO IV.

YOUNG Juan and his lady-love were left
  To their own hearts' most sweet society;
Even Time the pitiless in sorrow cleft
  With his rude scythe such gentle bosoms ; he
Sigh'd to behold them of their hours bereft,
  Though foe to love ; and yet they could not be
Meant to grow old, but die in happy spring,
Before one charm or hope had taken wing.

Their faces were not made for wrinkles, their
  Pure blood to stagnate, their great hearts to fail ;
The blank grey was not made to blast their hair,
  But like the climes that know nor snow nor hail,
They were all summer ; lightning might assail
  And shiver them to ashes, but to trail
A long and snake-like life of dull decay
Was not for them—they had too little clay.

They were alone once more ; for them to be
  Thus was another Eden ; they were never
Weary, unless when separate : the tree
  Cut from its forest root of years—the river
Damm'd from its fountain—the child from the knee
  And breast maternal wean'd at once for ever,—
Would wither less than these two torn apart ;
Alas ! there is no instinct like the heart—

The heart—which may be broken : happy they !
  Thrice fortunate ! who of that fragile mould,
The precious porcelain of human clay,
  Break with the first fall : they can ne'er behold
The long year link'd with heavy day on day,
  And all which must be borne, and never told ;
While life's strange principle will often lie
Deepest in those who long the most to die.

" Whom the gods love die young " was said of yore,
  And many deaths do they escape by this :
The death of friends, and that which slays even more—
  The death of friendship, love, youth, all that is,
Except mere breath ; and since the silent shore
  ` Awaits at last even those who longest miss
The old archer's shafts, perhaps the early grave
Which men weep over may be meant to save.

Haidée and Juan thought not of the dead.   [them:
    The heavens, and earth, and air, seem'd made for
They found no fault with Time, save that he fled;
    They saw not in themselves aught to condemn;
Each was the other's mirror, and but read
    Joy sparkling in their dark eyes like a gem,
And knew such brightness was but the reflection
Of their exchanging glances of affection.

The gentle pressure, and the thrilling touch,
    The least glance better understood than words,
Which still said all, and ne'er could say too much; ˙
    A language, too, but like to that of birds,
Known but to them, at least appearing such
    As but to lovers a true sense affords;
Sweet playful phrases, which would seem absurd
To those who have ceased to hear such, or ne'er heard.

All these were theirs, for they were children still,
    And children still they should have ever been;
They were not made in the real world to fill
    A busy character in the dull scene,
But like two beings born from out a rill,
    A nymph and her beloved, all unseen
To pass their lives in fountains and on flowers,
And never know the weight of human hours.

Moons changing had roll'd on, and changeless found
  Those their bright rise had lighted to such joys
As rarely they beheld throughout their round;
  And these were not of the vain kind which cloys,
For theirs were buoyant spirits, never bound
  By the mere senses; and that which destroys
Most love, possession, unto them appear'd
A thing which each endearment more endear'd.

From THE SAME.—CANTO IV.
THEY gazed upon the sunset; 'tis an hour
  Dear unto all, but dearest to *their* eyes,
For it had made them what they were : the power
  Of love had first o'erwhelm'd them from such skies,
When happiness had been their only dower,
  And twilight saw them link'd in passion's ties;
Charm'd with each other, all things charm'd that brought
The past still welcome as the present thought.

I know not why, but in that hour to-night,
  Even as they gazed, a sudden tremor came,
And swept, as 'twere, across their hearts' delight,
  Like the wind o'er a harp-string, or a flame,
When one is shook in sound, and one in sight :
  And thus some boding flash'd through either frame,
And call'd from Juan's breast a faint low sigh,
While one new tear arose in Haidée's eye.

That large black prophet eye seem'd to dilate
    And follow far the disappearing sun,
As if their last day of a happy date
    With his broad, bright, and dropping orb were gone.
Juan gazed on her as to ask his fate—
    He felt a grief, but knowing cause for none,
His glance inquired of hers for some excuse
For feelings causeless, or at least abstruse.

She turn'd to him, and smiled, but in that sort
    Which makes not others smile; then turn'd aside:
Whatever feeling shook her, it seem'd short,
    And master'd by her wisdom or her pride;
When Juan spoke, too—it might be in sport—
    Of this their mutual feeling, she replied—
" If it should be so,—but—it cannot be—
Or I at least shall not survive to see."

Juan would question further, but she press'd
    His lip to hers, and silenced him with this,
And then dismiss'd the omen from her breast,
    Defying augury with that fond kiss;
And no doubt of all methods 'tis the best:
    Some people prefer wine—'tis not amiss;
I have tried both; so those who would a part take
May choose between the headache and the heartache.

One of the two according to your choice,
  Woman or wine, you'll have to undergo ;
Both maladies are taxes on our joys :
  But which to choose, I really hardly know ;
And if I had to give a casting voice,
  For both sides I could many reasons show,
And then decide, without great wrong to either,
It were much better to have both than neither.

Juan and Haidée gazed upon each other
  With swimming looks of speechless tenderness,
Which mix'd all feelings, friend, child, lover, brother ;
  All that the best can mingle and express
When two pure hearts are pour'd in one another,
  And love too much, and yet cannot love less ;
But almost sanctify the sweet excess
By the immortal wish and power to bless.

Mix'd in each other's arms, and heart in heart,
  Why did they not then die ?—they had lived too long
Should an hour come to bid them breathe apart ;
  Years could but bring them cruel things or wrong ;
The world was not for them, nor the world's art
  For beings passionate as Sappho's song ;
Love was born *with* them, *in* them, so intense,
It was their very spirit—not a sense.

They should have lived together deep in woods,
  Unseen as sings the nightingale ; they were
Unfit to mix in these thick solitudes
  Call'd social, haunts of Hate, and Vice, and Care ;
How lonely every freeborn creature broods !
  The sweetest song-birds nestle in a pair ;
The eagle soars alone ; the gull and crow
Flock o'er their carrion, just like men below.

Now pillow'd cheek to cheek, in loving sleep,
  Haidée and Juan their siesta took,
A gentle slumber, but it was not deep,
  For ever and anon a something shook
Juan, and shuddering o'er his frame would creep ;
  And Haidée's sweet lips murmur'd like a brook
A wordless music, and her face so fair
Stirr'd with her dream, as rose-leaves with the air ;

Or as the stirring of a deep clear stream
  Within an Alpine hollow, when the wind
Walks o'er it, was she shaken by the dream,
  The mystical usurper of the mind—
O'erpowering us to be whate'er may seem
  Good to the soul which we no more can bind :
Strange state of being ! (for 'tis still to be),
Senseless to feel, and with seal'd eyes to see.

She dream'd of being alone on the sea-shore,
  Chain'd to a rock ; she knew not how, but stir
She could not from the spot, and the loud roar
  Grew, and each wave rose roughly, threatening her;
And o'er her upper lip they seem'd to pour,
  Until she sobb'd for breath, and soon they were
Foaming o'er her lone head, so fierce and high—
Each broke to drown her, yet she could not die.

Anon—she was released, and then she stray'd
  O'er the sharp shingles with her bleeding feet,
And stumbled almost every step she made ;
  And something roll'd before her in a sheet,
Which she must still pursue howe'er afraid :
  'Twas white and indistinct, nor stopp'd to meet
Her glance nor grasp, for still she gazed and grasp'd,
And ran, but it escaped her as she clasp'd.

The dream changed :—in a cave she stood, its walls
  Were hung with marble icicles ; the work
Of ages on its water-fretted halls,   [lurk ;
  Where waves might wash, and seals might breed and
Her hair was dripping, and the very balls
  Of her black eyes seem'd turn'd to tears, and mirk
The sharp rocks look'd below each drop they caught,
Which froze to marble as it fell,—she thought.

N

And wet, and cold, and lifeless at her feet,
    Pale as the foam that froth'd on his dead brow,
Which she essay'd in vain to clear, (how sweet
    Were once her cares, how idle seem'd they now !)
Lay Juan, nor could aught renew the beat
    Of his quench'd heart ; and the sea dirges low
Rang in her sad ears like a mermaid's song,
And that brief dream appear'd a life too long.

And gazing on the dead, she thought his face
    Faded, or alter'd into something new—
Like to her father's features, till each trace
    More like and like to Lambro's aspect grew—
With all his keen worn look and Grecian grace ;
    And starting, she awoke, and what to view? [there?
Oh ! Powers of Heaven ! what dark eye meets she
Tis—'tis her father's—fix'd upon the pair !

From THE SAME.—CANTO IV.

AFRIC is all the sun's, and as her earth
    Her human clay is kindled ; full of power
For good or evil, burning from its birth,
    The Moorish blood partakes the planet's hour,
And like the soil beneath it will bring forth :
    Beauty and love were Haidée's mother's dower ;
But her large dark eye show'd deep Passion's force,
Though sleeping like a lion near a source.

Her daughter, temper'd with a milder ray,
    Like summer clouds all silvery, smooth, and fair,
Till slowly charged with thunder they display
    Terror to earth, and tempest to the air,
Had held till now her soft and milky way;
    But overwrought with passion and despair,
The fire burst forth from her Numidian veins,
Even as the Simoom sweeps the blasted plains.

The last sight which she saw was Juan's gore,
    And he himself o'ermaster'd and cut down;
His blood was running on the very floor
    Where late he trod, her beautiful, her own;
Thus much she view'd an instant and no more,—
    Her struggles ceased with one convulsive groan;
On her sire's arm, which until now scarce held
Her writhing, fell she like a cedar fell'd.

A vein had burst, and her sweet lips' pure dyes
    Were dabbled with the deep blood which ran o'er;
And her head droop'd, as when the lily lies   [bore
    O'ercharged with rain: her summon'd handmaids
Their lady to her couch with gushing eyes;
    Of herbs and cordials they produced their store,
But she defied all means they could employ,
Like one life could not hold, nor death destroy.

Days lay she in that state unchanged, though chill—
    With nothing livid, still her lips were red ;
She had no pulse, but death seem'd absent still ;
    No hideous sign proclaim'd her surely dead ;
Corruption came not in each mind to kill
    All hope ; to look upon her sweet face bred
New thoughts of life, for it seem'd full of soul—
She had so much, earth could not claim the whole.

The ruling passion, such as marble shows
    When exquisitely chisell'd, still lay there,
But fix'd as marble's unchanged aspect throws
    O'er the fair Venus, but for ever fair ;
O'er the Laocoön's all eternal throes,
    And ever-dying Gladiator's air,
Their energy like life forms all their fame,
Yet looks not life, for they are still the same.

She woke at length, but not as sleepers wake,
    Rather the dead, for life seem'd something new,
A strange sensation which she must partake
    Perforce, since whatsoever met her view
Struck not on memory, though a heavy ache
    Lay at her heart, whose earliest beat still true
Brought back the sense of pain without the cause,
For, for a while, the furies made a pause.

She look'd on many a face with vacant eye,
  On many a token without knowing what;
She saw them watch her without asking why,
  And reck'd not who around her pillow sat;
Not speechless, though she spoke not; not a sigh
  Relieved her thoughts; dull silence and quick chat
Were tried in vain by those who served; she gave
No sign, save breath, of having left the grave.

Her handmaids tended, but she heeded not;
  Her father watch'd, she turned her eyes away;
She recognised no being, and no spot,
  However dear or cherish'd in their day;
They changed from room to room, but all forgot,
  Gentle, but without memory she lay;
At length those eyes, which they would fain be weaning
Back to old thoughts, wax'd full of fearful meaning.

And then a slave bethought her of a harp;
  The harper came, and tuned his instrument;
At the first notes, irregular and sharp,
  On him her flashing eyes a moment bent,
Then to the wall she turn'd as if to warp
  Her thoughts from sorrow through her heart re-sent;
And he began a long low island song
Of ancient days, ere tyranny grew strong.

Anon her thin wan fingers beat the wall
    In time to his old tune ; he changed the theme,
And sung of love ; the fierce name struck through all
    Her recollection ; on her flash'd the dream
Of what she was, and is, if ye could call
    To be so being ; in a gushing stream
The tears rush'd forth from her o'erclouded brain,
Like mountain mists at length dissolved in rain.

Short solace, vain relief !—thought came too quick,
    And whirl'd her brain to madness ; she arose
As one who ne'er had dwelt among the sick,
    And flew at all she met, as on her foes ;
But no one ever heard her speak or shriek,
    Although her paroxysm drew towards its close ;—
Hers was a phrensy which disdain'd to rave,
Even when they smote her, in the hope to save.

Yet she betray'd at times a gleam of sense ;
    Nothing could make her meet her father's face,
Though on all other things with looks intense
    She gazed, but none she ever could retrace ;
Food she refused, and raiment ; no pretence
    Avail'd for either ; neither change of place,
Nor time, nor skill, nor remedy, could give her
Senses to sleep—the power seem'd gone for ever.

Twelve days and nights she wither'd thus; at last,
    Without a groan, or sigh, or glance, to show
A parting pang, the spirit from her passed:
    And they who watch'd her nearest could not know
The very instant, till the change that cast
    Her sweet face into shadow, dull and slow,
Glazed o'er her eyes—the beautiful, the black—
Oh! to possess such lustre—and then lack!

She died, but not alone; she held within
    A second principle of life, which might
Have dawn'd a fair and sinless child of sin;
    But closed its little being without light,
And went down to the grave unborn, wherein
    Blossom and bough lie wither'd with one blight;
In vain the dews of Heaven descend above
The bleeding flower and blasted fruit of love.

Thus lived—thus died she; never more on her
    Shall sorrow light, or shame. She was not made
Through years or moons the inner weight to bear,
    Which colder hearts endure till they are laid
By age in earth: her days and pleasures were
    Brief, but delightful—such as had not staid
Long with her destiny; but she sleeps well
By the sea-shore, whereon she loved to dwell.

That isle is now all desolate and bare,
 Its dwellings down, its tenants pass'd away ; ·
None but her own and father's grave is there,
 And nothing outward tells of human clay ;
Ye could not know where lies a thing so fair,
 No stone is there to show, no tongue to say,
What was ; no dirge, except the hollow sea's,
Mourns o'er the beauty of the Cyclades.

But many a Greek maid in a loving song
 Sighs o'er her name ; and many an islander
With her sire's story makes the night less long ;
 Valour was his, and beauty dwelt with her ;
If she loved rashly, her life paid for wrong—
 A heavy price must all pay who thus err,
In some shape ; let none think to fly the danger,
For soon or late Love is his own avenger.

From THE SAME.—CANTO XIII.

IT stood embosom'd in a happy valley,
 Crown'd by high woodlands, where the Druid oak
Stood, like Caractacus, in act to rally
 His host, with broad arms 'gainst the thunderstroke,
And from beneath his boughs were seen to sally
 The dappled foresters ; as day awoke,
The branching stag swept down with all his herd,
To quaff a brook which murmur'd like a bird.

Before the mansion lay a lucid lake,
  Broad as transparent, deep, and freshly fed
By a river, which its soften'd way did take
  In currents through the calmer water spread
Around : the wildfowl nestled in the brake
  And sedges, brooding in their liquid bed :
The woods sloped downwards to its brink, and stood
With their green faces fix'd upon the flood.

Its outlet dash'd into a deep cascade,
  Sparkling with foam, until again subsiding,
Its shriller echoes—like an infant made
  Quiet—sank into softer ripples, gliding
Into a rivulet : and thus allay'd,
  Pursued its course, now gleaming, and now hiding
Its windings through the woods; now clear, now blue,
According as the skies their shadows threw.

A glorious remnant of the Gothic pile
  (While yet the church was Rome's) stood half apart
In a grand arch, which once screen'd many an aisle.
  These last had disappear'd—a loss to art :
The first yet frown'd superbly o'er the soil,
  And kindled feelings in the roughest heart,
Which mourn'd the power of time's or tempest's march,
In gazing on that venerable arch.

Within a niche, nigh to its pinnacle,
  Twelve saints had once stood sanctified in stone ;
But these had fallen, not when the friars fell,
  But in the war which struck Charles from his throne,
When each house was a fortalice—as tell
  The annals of full many a line undone,—
The gallant cavaliers, who fought in vain
For those who knew not to resign or reign.

But in a higher niche, alone, but crown'd,
  The Virgin-Mother of the God-born Child,
With her Son in her blessed arms, look'd round ;
  Spared by some chance when all beside was spoil'd ;
She made the earth below seem holy ground.
  This may be superstition, weak or wild,
But even the faintest relics of a shrine
Of any worship wake some thoughts divine.

A mighty window, hollow in the centre,
  Shorn of its glass of thousand colourings,
Through which the deepen'd glories once could enter,
  Streaming from off the sun like seraph's wings,
Now yawns all desolate : now loud, now fainter,
  The gale sweeps through its fretwork, and oft sings
The owl his anthem, where the silenced quire
Lie with their hallelujahs quench'd like fire.

But in the noontide of the moon, and when
  The wind is winged from one point of heaven,
There moans a strange unearthly sound, which then
  Is musical—a dying accent driven
Through the huge arch, which soars and sinks again.
  Some deem it but the distant echo given
Back to the night-wind by the waterfall,
And harmonised by the old choral wall;

Others, that some original shape, or form
  Shaped by decay perchance, hath given the power
(Though less than that of Memnon's statue, warm
  In Egypt's rays, to harp at a fix'd hour)
To this grey ruin, with a voice to charm
  Sad, but serene, it sweeps o'er tree or tower;
The cause I know not, nor can solve; but such
The fact:—I've heard it,—once perhaps too much.

From THE SAME.—CANTO XV.

BETWEEN two worlds life hovers like a star,
  'Twixt night and morn, upon the horizon's verge.
How little do we know that which we are!
  How less what we may be! The eternal surge
Of time and tide rolls on, and bears afar
  Our bubbles; as the old burst, new emerge,
Lash'd from the foam of ages; while the graves
Of empires heave but like some passing waves.

From "*HEAVEN AND EARTH.*"

Anah.   SERAPH !
From thy sphere !
Whatever star contain thy glory ;
  In the eternal depths of heaven
  Albeit thou watchest with "the seven,"
Though through space infinite and hoary
  Before thy bright wings worlds be driven,
                    Yet hear !
Oh ! think of her who holds thee dear !
And though she nothing is to thee,
Yet think that thou art all to her.
  Thou canst not tell,—and never be
  Such pangs decreed to aught save me,—
    The bitterness of tears.
    Eternity is in thine years,
Unborn, undying beauty in thine eyes ;
With me thou canst not sympathise,

Except in love, and there thou must
    Acknowledge that more loving dust
Ne'er wept beneath the skies.
Thou walk'st thy many worlds, thou see'st
    The face of him who made thee great,
As he hath made me of the least
    Of those cast out from Eden's gate ;
        Yet, Seraph dear !
          Oh hear !
For thou hast loved me, and I would not die
    Until I know what I must die in knowing,
That thou forgett'st in thine eternity
    Her whose heart death could not keep from
        o'erflowing
For thee, immortal essence as thou art !
    Great is their love who love in sin and fear ;
And such, I feel, are waging in my heart
A war unworthy : to an Adamite
    Forgive, my Seraph ! that such thoughts appear,
      For sorrow is our element ; '
         Delight
An Eden kept afar from sight,
      Though sometimes with our visions blent.
      The hour is near
Which tells me we are not abandon'd quite.—
      Appear ! Appear !

Seraph !
My own Azaziel ! be but here,
And leave the stars to their own light.
Aholibamah.   Samiasa !
Wheresoe'er
Thou rulest in the upper air—
Or warring with the spirits who may dare
Dispute with him
Who made all empires, empire; or recalling
Some wandering star, which shoots through the abyss,
Whose tenants dying, while their world is falling,
Share the dim destiny of clay in this;
Or joining with the inferior cherubim,
Thou deignest to partake their hymn—
Samiasa !
I call thee, I await thee, and I love thee.
Many may worship thee, that will I not :
If that thy spirit down to mine may move thee,
Descend and share my lot !
Though I be form'd of clay,
And thou of beams
More bright than those of day
On Eden's streams,
Thine immortality cannot repay
With love more warm than mine
My love.   There is a ray

In me, which, though forbidden yet to shine,
 I feel was lighted at thy God's and thine.
It may be hidden long : death and decay
 Our mother Eve bequeath'd us—but my heart
Defies it : though this life must pass away,
 Is *that* a cause for thee and me to part ?
Thou art immortal—so am I : I feel—
 I feel my immortality o'ersweep
All pains, all tears, all time, all fears, and peal,
 Like the eternal thunders of the deep,
Into my ears this truth—" Thou liv'st for ever ! "
    But if it be in joy
 I know not, nor would know ;
That secret rests with the Almighty giver,
 Who folds in clouds the fonts of bliss and woe.
    But thee and me he never can destroy ;
 Change us he may, but not o'erwhelm ; we are
Of as eternal essence, and must war
With him if he will war with us : with thee
 I can share all things, even immortal sorrow ;
For thou hast ventured to share life with me,
And shall I shrink from thine eternity ?
    No ! though the serpent's sting should pierce me
        thorough,
And thou thyself wert like the serpent, coil
Around me still ! and I will smile,

And curse thee not ; but hold
Thee in as warm a fold
As—— but descend, and prove
A mortal's love
For an immortal.   If the skies contain
More joy than thou canst give and take, remain !
 Anah. Sister! sister! I view them winging
Their bright way through the parted night.
 Aho. The clouds from off their pinions flinging,
As though they bore to-morrow's light.
 Anah. But if our father see the sight !
 Aho. He would but deem it was the moon
Rising unto some sorcerer's tune
An hour too soon.
 Anah. They come ! *he* comes !—Azaziel !
 Aho.   Haste
To meet them !   Oh ! for wings to bear
My spirit, while they hover there,
To Samiasa's breast !
 Anah. Lo ! they have kindled all the west,
Like a returning sunset ;—lo !
On Ararat's late secret crest
A mild and many-colour'd bow,
The remnant of their flashing path,
Now shines ! and now, behold ! it hath
Return'd to night, as rippling foam,

Which the leviathan hath lash'd
From his unfathomable home,
When sporting on the face of the calm deep,
  Subsides soon after he again hath dash'd
Down, down, to where the ocean's fountains sleep.

From THE SAME.—PART I., SCENE III.

Spirit.   REJOICE !
    The abhorrèd race
Which could not keep in Eden their high place,
    But listen'd to the voice
Of knowledge without power,
    Are nigh the hour
    Of death !
Not slow, not single, not by sword, nor sorrow,
  Nor years, nor heart-break, nor time's sapping motion,
Shall they drop off.   Behold their last to-morrow !
    Earth shall be ocean !
    And no breath,
Save of the winds, be on the unbounded wave !
  Angels shall tire their wings, but find no spot :
Not even a rock from out the liquid grave
    Shall lift its point to save,
Or show the place where strong Despair hath died,

        O

After long looking o'er the ocean wide
    For the expected ebb which cometh not:
        All shall be void,
            Destroy'd!
Another element shall be the lord
    Of life, and the abhorr'd
Children of dust be quench'd; and of each hue
Of earth nought left but the unbroken blue;
    And of the variegated mountain
        Shall nought remain
        Unchanged, or of the level plain;
        Cedar and pine shall lift their tops in vain:
All merged within the universal fountain,
Man, earth, and fire, shall die,
        And sea and sky
Look vast and lifeless in the eternal eye.
        Upon the foam
        Who shall erect a home?
Japhet (coming forward). My sire!
    Earth's seed shall not expire;
    Only the evil shall be put away
        From day.
Avaunt! ye exulting demons of the waste!
    Who howl your hideous joy
When God destroys whom you dare not destroy;
        Hence! haste!

Back to your inner caves !
Until the waves
Shall search you in your secret place,
And drive your sullen race
Forth, to be roll'd upon the tossing winds,
    In restless wretchedness along all space !
Spirit.   Son of the saved !
    When thou and thine have braved
    The wide and warring element;
When the great barrier of the deep is rent,
Shall thou and thine be good or happy ?—No !
Thy new world and new race shall be of woe—
    Less goodly in their aspect, in their years
        Less than the glorious giants, who
        Yet walk the world in pride,
The Sons of·Heaven by many a mortal bride.
    Thine shall be nothing of the past, save tears.
        And art thou not ashamed
        Thus to survive,
        And eat, and drink, and wive ?
With a base heart so far subdued and tamed,
As even to hear this wide destruction named,
Without such grief and courage, as should rather
    Bid thee await the world-dissolving wave,
Than seek a shelter with thy favour'd father,
    And build thy city o'er the drown'd earth's grave ?

Who would outlive their kind,
Except the base and blind?
Mine
Hateth thine
As of a different order in the sphere,
But not our own.
There is not one who hath not left a throne
Vacant in heaven to dwell in darkness here,
Rather than see his mates endure alone.
Go, wretch! and give
A life like thine to other wretches—live!
And when the annihilating waters roar
Above what they have done,
Envy the giant patriarchs then no more,
And scorn thy sire as the surviving one!
Thyself for being his son!

Chorus of Spirits issuing from the cavern.

Rejoice!
No more the human voice
Shall vex our joys in middle air
With prayer;
No more
Shall they adore;
And we, who ne'er for ages have adored
The prayer-exacting Lord,

To whom the omission of a sacrifice
    Is vice;
We, we shall view the deep's salt sources pour'd
Until one element shall do the work
    Of all in chaos; until they,
    The creatures proud of their poor clay,
Shall perish, and their bleached bones shall lurk
In caves, in dens, in clefts of mountains, where
The deep shall follow to their latest lair;
Where even the brutes, in their despair,
Shall cease to prey on man and on each other,
    And the striped tiger shall lie down to die
Beside the lamb, as though he were his brother;
    Till all things shall be as they were,
    Silent and uncreated, save the sky:
    While a brief truce
Is made with Death, who shall forbear
The little remnant of the past creation,
    To generate new nations for his use;
This remnant, floating o'er the undulation
Of the subsiding deluge, from its slime,
When the hot sun hath baked the reeking soil
Into a world, shall give again to Time
New beings—years, diseases, sorrow, crime—
With all companionship of hate and toil,
    Until——

Japh. (*interrupting them*). The eternal will
  Shall deign to expound this dream
  Of good and evil ; and redeem
      Unto himself all times, all things ;
      And, gather'd under his almighty wings,
          Abolish hell !
  And to the expiated Earth
  Restore the beauty of her birth,
      Her Eden in an endless paradise,
  Where man no more can fall as once he fell,
  And even the very demons shall do well !
Spirits. And when shall take effect this wondrous
      spell ?
Japh. When the Redeemer cometh ; first in pain,
      And then in glory.
Spirit. Meantime still struggle in the mortal chain,
      Till earth wax hoary :
War with yourselves, and hell, and heaven, in vain,
      Until the clouds look gory
With the blood reeking from each battle plain ;
New times, new climes, new arts, new men ; but still,
The same old tears, old crimes, and oldest ill,
Shall be amongst your race in different forms ;
      But the same moral storms
  Shall oversweep the future, as the waves
  In a few hours the glorious giants' graves.

Chorus of Spirits.

Brethren, rejoice !
Mortal, farewell !
Hark ! hark ! already we can hear the voice
  Of growing ocean's gloomy swell ;
  The winds, too, plume their piercing wings ;
  The clouds have nearly fill'd their springs ;
The fountains of the great deep shall be broken,
  And heaven set wide her windows ; while mankind
View, unacknowledged, each tremendous token—
  Still, as they were from the beginning, blind.
  We hear the sound they cannot hear,
  The mustering thunders of the threatening sphere ;
  Yet a few hours their coming is delay'd ;
  Their flashing banners, folded still on high,
      Yet undisplay'd,
  Save to the Spirit's all-pervading eye.
    Howl ! howl ! oh Earth !
Thy death is nearer than thy recent birth ;
Tremble, ye mountains, soon to shrink below
    The ocean's overflow !
The wave shall break upon your cliffs ; and shells,
  The little shells, of ocean's least things be
Deposed where now the eagle's offspring dwells—
  How shall he shriek o'er the remorseless sea !

And call his nestlings up with fruitless yell,
Unanswer'd, save by the encroaching swell ;—
While man shall long in vain for his broad wings,
   The wings which could not save :—
Where could he rest them, while the whole space brings
   Nought to his eye beyond the deep, his grave ?
        Brethren, rejoice !
And loudly lift each superhuman voice—
        All die,
Save the slight remnant of Seth's seed—
      The seed of Seth,
Exempt for future sorrow's sake from death.
     But of the sons of Cain
     None shall remain ;
   And all his goodly daughters
  Must lie beneath the desolating waters ;
Or, floating upward, with their long hair laid
Along the wave, the cruel heaven upbraid,
     Which would not spare
     Beings even in death so fair.
     It is decreed,
      All die !
And to the universal human cry
The universal silence shall succeed !
     Fly, brethren, fly !
     But still rejoice !

We fell!
They fall!
So perish all
These petty foes of Heaven who shrink from hell!

From THE SAME.—PART I., SCENE III.

Raphael. SPIRITS!
  Whose seat is near the throne,
    What do ye here?
Is thus a seraph's duty to be shown,
    Now that the hour is near
When earth must be alone?
    Return!
  Adore and burn,
In glorious homage with the elected "seven."
    Your place is heaven.
Samiasa. Raphael!
The first and fairest of the sons of God,
    How long hath this been law,
That earth by angels must be left untrod?
    Earth! which oft saw
Jehovah's footsteps not disdain her sod!
  The world he loved, and made
  For love; and oft have we obey'd
His frequent mission with delighted pinions:

Adoring him in his least works display'd ;
Watching this youngest star of his dominions ;
And, as the latest birth of his great word,
Eager to keep it worthy of our Lord.
Why is thy brow severe ?
And wherefore speak'st thou of destruction near ?
Raph. Had Samiasa and Azaziel been
In their true place, with the angelic choir,
Written in fire
They would have seen
Jehovah's late decree,
And not inquired their Maker's breath of me :
But ignorance must ever be
A part of sin ;
And even the spirits' knowledge shall grow less
As they wax proud within ;
For Blindness is the first-born of Excess.
When all good angels left the world, ye stay'd,
Stung with strange passions, and debased
By mortal feelings for a mortal maid :
But ye are pardon'd thus far, and replaced
With your pure equals.   Hence ! away ! away !
Or stay,
And lose eternity by that delay !
Azaziel. And thou ! if earth be thus forbidden
In the decree

    To us until this moment hidden,
        Dost thou not err as we
          In being here?
Raph. I came to call ye back to your fit sphere,
  In the great name and at the word of God.
Dear, dearest in themselves, and scarce less dear
  That which I came to do : till now we trod
'Together the eternal space ; together
  Let us still walk the stars.   True, earth must die!
Her race, return'd into her womb, must wither,
    And much which she inherits : but oh ! why
      Cannot this earth be made, or be destroy'd,
      Without involving ever some vast void
In the immortal ranks? immortal still
    In their immeasurable forfeiture.
Our brother Satan fell ; his burning will
    Rather than longer worship dared endure !
      But ye who still are pure !
Seraphs ! less mighty than that mightiest one,
    Think how he was undone !
And think if tempting man can compensate
  For heaven desired too late ?
        Long have I warr'd,
        Long must I war
      With him who deem'd it hard
    To be created, and to acknowledge him

Who midst the cherubim
    Made him as suns to a dependent star,
Leaving the archangels at his right hand dim.
    I loved him—beautiful he was : oh, heaven !
Save *his* who made, what beauty and what power
Was ever like to Satan's !   Would the hour
    In which he fell could ever be forgiven !
The wish is impious : but, oh ye !
Yet undestroy'd, be warn'd !   Eternity
    With him, or with his God, is in your choice :
He hath not tempted you ; he cannot tempt
The angels, from his further snares exempt :
    But man hath listen'd to his voice,
And ye to woman's—beautiful she is,
The serpent's voice less subtle than her kiss.
The snake but vanquish'd dust ; but she will draw
A second host from heaven, to break heaven's law.
                    Yet, yet, oh fly !
                    Ye cannot die ;
                    But they
                    Shall pass away,
While ye shall fill with shrieks the upper sky
            For perishable clay,
Whose memory in your immortality
    Shall long outlast the sun which gave them day.
Think how your essence differeth from theirs

In all but suffering ! why partake
The agony to which they must be heirs—
Born to be plough'd with years, and sown with cares,
   And reap'd by Death, lord of the human soil?
Even had their days been left to toil their path
Through time to dust, unshorten'd by God's wrath,
   Still they are Evil's prey and Sorrow's spoil.
   Aho.   Let them fly !
I hear the voice which says that all must die,
Sooner than our white-bearded patriarchs died ;
        And that on high
       An ocean is prepared,
       While from below
The deep shall rise to meet heaven's overflow.
       Few shall be spared,
It seems ; and, of that few, the race of Cain
Must lift their eyes to Adam's God in vain.
      Sister ! since it is so,
     And the eternal Lord
     In vain would be implored
For the remission of one hour of woe,
Let us resign even what we have adored,
And meet the wave, as we would meet the sword,
   If not unmoved, yet undismay'd,
And wailing less for us than those who shall
Survive in mortal or immortal thrall,

And, when the fatal waters are allay'd,
Weep for the myriads who can weep no more.
Fly, seraphs ! to your own eternal shore,
Where winds nor howl nor waters roar.
          Our portion is to die,
          And yours to live for ever :
But which is best, a dead eternity,
Or living, is but known to the great Giver.
          Obey him, as we shall obey ;
I would not keep this life of mine in clay
          An hour beyond his will ;
Nor see ye lose a portion of his grace,
For all the mercy which Seth's race
          Find still.
          Fly !
And as your pinions bear ye back to heaven,
Think that my love still mounts with thee on high,
          Samiasa !
And if I look up with a tearless eye,
'Tis that an angel's bride disdains to weep,—
Farewell,! Now rise, inexorable deep !
Anah.   And must we die ?
          And must I lose thee too,
          Azaziel ?
     Oh, my heart ! my heart !
     Thy prophecies were true !

And yet thou wert so happy too !
The blow, though not unlook'd for, falls as new :
But yet depart !
Ah ! why ?
Yet let me not retain thee—fly !
My pangs can be but brief ; but thine would be
Eternal, if repulsed from heaven for me.
Too much already hast thou deign'd
To one of Adam's race !
Our doom is sorrow : not to us alone,
But to the spirits who have not disdain'd
To love us, cometh anguish with disgrace.
The first who taught us knowledge hath been hurl'd
From his once archangelic throne
Into some unknown world :
And thou, Azaziel ! No—
Thou shalt not suffer woe
For me. Away ! nor weep !
Thou canst not weep ; but yet
May'st suffer more, not weeping : then forget
Her, whom the surges of the all-strangling deep
Can bring no pang like this. Fly ! fly !
Being gone, 'twill be less difficult to die.
Japh. Oh, say not so !
Father ! and thou, archangel, thou !
Surely celestial mercy lurks below

That pure severe serenity of brow :
Let them not meet this sea without a shore,
Save in our ark, or let me be no more !
Noah. Peace, child of passion, peace !
If not within thy heart, yet with thy tongue
  Do God no wrong !
Live as he wills it—die, when he ordains,
A righteous death, unlike the seed of Cain's.
 Cease, or be sorrowful in silence ; cease
To weary Heaven's ear with thy selfish plaint.
 Wouldst thou have God commit a sin for thee ?
   Such would it be
   To alter his intent
For a mere mortal sorrow.   Be a man !
And bear what Adam's race must bear, and can.
 Japh. Ay, father ! but when they are gone,
   And we are all alone,
Floating upon the azure desert, and
The depth beneath us hides our own dear land,
 And dearer, silent friends and brethren, all
 Buried in its immeasurable breast,
Who, who, our tears, our shrieks, shall then command ?
 Can we in desolation's peace have rest ?   ·
  Oh God ! be thou a God, and spare
   Yet while 'tis time ;
   Renew not Adam's fall :

Mankind were then but twain,
But they are numerous now as are the waves
And the tremendous rain,
Whose drops shall be less thick than would their graves,
Were graves permitted to the seed of Cain.
Noah. Silence, vain boy! each word of thine's a crime,
Angel! forgive this stripling's fond despair.
Raph. Seraphs! these mortals speak in passion: Ye!
Who are, or should be, passionless and pure,
May now return with me.
Sam.   It may not be:
We have chosen, and will endure.
Raph. Say'st thou?
Aza.   He hath said it, and I say, Amen!
Raph.   Again!
    Then from this hour,
    Shorn as ye are of all celestial power,
    And aliens from your God,
                Farewell!
Japh.   Alas! where shall they dwell?
Hark, hark! Deep sounds, and deeper still,
    Are howling from the mountain's bosom:
There's not a breath of wind upon the hill,
    Yet quivers every leaf, and drops each blossom:
Earth groans as if beneath a heavy load.
Noah. Hark, hark! the sea-birds cry!

P

In clouds they overspread the lurid sky,
And hover round the mountain, where before
Never a white wing, wetted by the wave,
        Yet dared to soar,
Even when the waters wax'd too fierce to brave.
    Soon it shall be their only shore,
        And then, no more !
Japh.   The sun ! the sun !
He riseth, but his better light is gone ;
        And a black circle, bound
        His glaring disk around,
Proclaims earth's last of summer days hath shone !
    The clouds return into the hues of night,
Save where their brazen-colour'd edges streak
The verge where brighter morns were wont to break.
    Noah. And lo ! yon flash of light,
The distant thunder's harbinger, appears !
    It cometh ! hence, away !
Leave to the elements their evil prey !
Hence to where our all-hallow'd ark uprears
        Its safe and wreckless sides !
Japh. Oh, father, stay !
Leave not my Anah to the swallowing tides !
    Noah. Must we not leave all life to such? Begone !
Japh.   Not I.
Noah.   Then die

With them !
How darest thou look on that prophetic sky,
And seek to save what all things now condemn,
    In overwhelming unison
        With just Jehovah's wrath !
Japh. Can rage and justice join in the same path?
Noah. Blasphemer! darest thou murmur even now?
Raph. Patriarch, be still a father! smooth thy brow:
Thy son, despite his folly, shall not sink :
He knows not what he says, yet shall not drink
    With sobs the salt foam of the swelling waters:
But be, when passion passeth, good as thou,
    Nor perish like heaven's children with man's
        daughters.
    Aho. The tempest cometh ; heaven and earth unite
    For the annihilation of all life.
    Unequal is the strife
Between our strength and the Eternal Might !
Sam. But ours is with thee ; we will bear ye far
    To some untroubled star,
Where thou and Anah shalt partake our lot :
    And if thou dost not weep for thy lost earth,
Our forfeit heaven shall also be forgot.
    Anah. Oh! my dear father's tents, my place of birth,
And mountains, land, and woods ! when ye are not,
Who shall dry up my tears ?

Aza. Thy spirit-lord.
Fear not; though we are shut from heaven,
Yet much is ours, whence we cannot be driven.
    Raph. Rebel! thy words are wicked, as thy deeds
Shall henceforth be but weak : the flaming sword,
Which chased the first-born out of Paradise,
Still flashes in the angelic hands.
    Aza. It cannot slay us : threaten dust with death,
And talk of weapons unto that which bleeds.
What are thy swords in our immortal eyes?
    Raph. The moment cometh to approve thy strength;
      And learn at length
How vain to war with what thy God commands :
Thy former force was in thy faith.

Enter Mortals, flying for refuge.

Chorus of Mortals.

The heavens and earth are mingling—God! oh God!
What have we done?   Yet spare!
Hark! even the forest beasts howl forth their prayer!
    The dragon crawls from out his den,
    To herd, in terror, innocent with men;
And the birds scream their agony through air.
Yet, yet, Jehovah! yet withdraw thy rod
Of wrath, and pity thine own world's·despair!
Hear not man only but all nature plead!

Raph. Farewell, thou earth! ye wretched sons of
clay,
I cannot, must not, aid you.   'Tis decreed!

[*Exit* RAPHAEL.

Japh. Some clouds sweep on as vultures for their
prey,
While others, fix'd as rocks, await the word
At which their wrathful vials shall be pour'd.
No azure more shall robe the firmament,
  Nor spangled stars be glorious : Death hath risen :
In the sun's place a pale and ghastly glare
Hath wound itself around the dying air.

Aza. Come, Anah! quit this chaos-founded prison,
To which the elements again repair,
To turn it into what it was : beneath
The shelter of these wings thou shalt be safe,
As was the eagle's nestling once within
Its mother's.—Let the coming chaos chafe
With all its elements !   Heed not their din !.
A brighter world than this, where thou shalt breathe
Ethereal life, will we explore :
These darken'd clouds are not the only skies.

[AZAZIEL *and* SAMIASA *fly off and disappear with*
ANAH *and* AHOLIBAMAH.

Japh. They are gone ! They have disappear'd amidst
the roar

Of the forsaken world ; and never more,
Whether they live, or die with all earth's life,
Now near its last, can aught restore
Anah unto these eyes.

Chorus of Mortals.

Oh son of Noah ! mercy on thy kind !
What ! wilt thou leave us all—all—*all* behind ?
While safe amidst the elemental strife,
Thou sitt'st within thy guarded ark ?
A Mother (offering her infant to JAPHET). Oh let
      this child embark !
   I brought him forth in woe,
         But thought it joy
   To see him to my bosom clinging so.
         Why was he born ?
         What hath he done—
         My unwean'd son—
To move Jehovah's wrath or scorn ?
What is there in this milk of mine, that death
   Should stir all heaven and earth up to destroy
         My boy,
And roll the waters o'er his placid breath ?
Save him, thou seed of Seth !
Or cursed be—with him who made
Thee and thy race, for which we are betray'd !

Japh. Peace ! 'tis no hour for curses, but for prayer !

Chorus of Mortals.

For prayer !
And where
Shall prayer ascend,
When the swoln clouds unto the mountains bend
And burst,
And gushing oceans every barrier rend,
Until the very deserts know no thirst
Accursed
Be he who made thee and thy sire !
We deem our curses vain ; we must expire ,
But as we know the worst,
Why should our hymn be raised, our knees be bent
Before the implacable Omnipotent,
Since we must fall the same ?
If he hath made earth, let it be his shame,
To make a world for torture.—Lo ! they come,
The loathsome waters, in their rage !
And with their roar make-wholesome nature dumb !
The forests' trees (coeval with the hour
When Paradise upsprung,
Ere Eve gave Adam knowledge for her dower,
Or Adam his first hymn of slavery sung),

So massy, vast, yet green in their old age,
    Are overtopp'd,
Their summer blossoms by the surges lopp'd,
Which rise, and rise, and rise.
Vainly we look up to the lowering skies—
    They meet the seas,
And shut out God from our beseeching eyes.
    Fly, son of Noah, fly ! and take thine ease,
In thine allotted ocean-tent ;
And view, all floating o'er the element,
The corpses of the world of thy young days :
        Then to Jehovah raise
        Thy song of praise !
A Mortal. Blessed are the dead
        Who die in the Lord !
And though the waters be o'er earth outspread,
        Yet, as *his* word,
        Be the decree adored !
He gave me life—he taketh but
    The breath which is his own :
And though these eyes should be for ever shut,
    Nor longer this weak voice before his throne
    Be heard in supplicating tone,
            Still blessed be the Lord,
            For what is past,
            For that which is :

For all are his,
From first to last—
Time, space, eternity, life, death—
The vast known and immeasurable unknown.
He made, and can unmake;
And shall *I*, for a little gasp of breath,
Blaspheme and groan?
No; let me die, as I have lived, in faith,
Nor quiver, though the universe may quake!

Chorus of Mortals.

Where shall we fly?
Not to the mountains high;
For now their torrents rush, with double roar,
To meet the ocean, which, advancing still,
Already grasps each drowning hill,
Nor leaves an unsearch'd cave.

Enter a Woman.

Woman. Oh, save me, save!
Our valley is no more:
My father and my father's tent,
My brethren and my brethren's herds,
The pleasant trees that o'er our noonday bent,
And sent forth evening songs from sweetest birds,
The little rivulet which freshen'd all

Our pastures green,
No more are to be seen.
When to the mountain cliff I climb'd this morn,
  I turn'd to bless the spot,
And not a leaf appear'd about to fall ;—
  And now they are not !
Why was I born ?
Japh.   To die ! in youth to die !
And happier in that doom,
Than to behold the universal tomb,
          Which I
Am thus condemn'd to weep above in vain.
Why, when all perish, why must I remain ?

From "*THE DEFORMED TRANSFORMED.*"

PART I., SCENE I.

BEAUTIFUL shadow
　Of Thetis's boy !
Who sleeps in the meadow
　Whose grass grows o'er Troy :
From the red earth, like Adam,
　Thy likeness I shape,
As the being who made him,
　Whose actions I ape.
Thou clay, be all glowing,
　Till the rose in his cheek
Be as fair as, when blowing,
　It wears its first streak !
Ye violets, I scatter,
　Now turn into eyes !
And thou, sunshiny water,
　Of blood take the guise !

Let these hyacinth boughs
  Be his long flowing hair,
And wave o'er his brows
  As thou wavest in air !
Let his heart be this marble
  I tear from the rock !
But his voice as the warble
  Of birds on yon oak !
Let his flesh be the purest
  Of mould, in which grew
The lily-root surest,
  And drank the best dew !
Let his limbs be the lightest
  Which clay can compound,
And his aspect the brightest
  On earth to be found !
Elements, near me,
  Be mingled and stirr'd,
Know me, and hear me,
  And leap to my word !
Sunbeams, awaken
  This earth's animation !
'Tis done !   He hath taken
  His stand in creation !

From THE SAME.—PART II., SCENE I.

Chorus of Spirits in the air.

'TIS the morn, but dim and dark,
Whither flies the silent lark?
Whither shrinks the clouded sun?
Is the day indeed begun?
Nature'e eye is melancholy
O'er the city high and holy:
But without there is a din
Should arouse the saints within,
And revive the heroic ashes
Round which yellow Tiber dashes.
Oh, ye seven hills! awaken,
Ere your very base be shaken!

Hearken to the steady stamp!
Mars is in their every tramp!
Not a step is out of tune!
As the tides obey the moon,
On they march, though to self-slaughter,
Regular as rolling water,
Whose high waves o'ersweep the border
Of huge moles, but keep their order,
Breaking only rank by rank.
Hearken to the armour's clank!

Look down o'er each frowning warrior,
How he glares upon the barrier :
Look on each step of each ladder,
As the stripes that streak an adder.

Look upon the bristling wall,
Mann'd without an interval !
Round and round, and tier on tier,
Cannon's black mouth, shining spear,
Lit match, bell-mouth'd musquetoon,
Gaping to be murderous soon ;
All the warlike gear of old,
Mix'd with what we now behold,
In this strife 'twixt old and new,
Gather like a locusts' crew.
Shade of Remus ! 'tis a time
Awful as thy brother's crime !
Christians war against Christ's shrine :—
Must its lot be like to thine ?

Near—and near—and nearer still,
As the earthquake saps the hill,
First with trembling, hollow motion,
Like a scarce awaken'd ocean,
Then with stronger shock and louder,
Till the rocks are crush'd to powder,—

Onward sweeps the rolling host !
Heroes of the immortal boast !
Mighty chiefs ! eternal shadows !
First flowers of the bloody meadows
Which encompass Rome, the mother
Of a people without brother !
Will you sleep when nations' quarrels
Plough the root up of your laurels ?
Ye who weep o'er Carthage burning,
Weep not—strike ! for Rome is mourning !

Onward sweep the varied nations !
Famine long hath dealt their rations.
To the wall, with hate and hunger,
Numerous as wolves, and stronger,
On they sweep.   Oh, glorious city !
Must thou be a theme for pity ?
Fight, like your first sire, each Roman !
Alaric was a gentle foeman,
Match'd with Bourbon's black banditti !
Rouse thee, thou eternal city ;
Rouse thee !   Rather give the torch
With thine own hand to thy porch,
Than behold such hosts pollute
Your worst dwelling with their foot.

Ah ! behold yon bleeding spectre !
Ilion's children find no Hector;
Priam's offspring loved their brother;
Rome's great sire forgot his mother,
When he slew his gallant twin,
With inexpiable sin.
See the giant shadow stride
O'er the ramparts high and wide !
When the first o'erleapt thy wall,
Its foundation mourn'd thy fall.
Now, though towering like a Babel,
Who to stop his steps are able ?
Stalking o'er thy highest dome,
Remus claims his vengeance, Rome !

Now they reach thee in their anger:
Fire and smoke and hellish clangour
Are around thee, thou world's wonder !
Death is in thy walls and under.
Now the meeting steel first clashes,
Downward then the ladder crashes,
With its iron load all gleaming,
Lying at its foot blaspheming !
Up again ! for every warrior
Slain, another climbs the barrier.
Thicker grows the strife : thy ditches

Europe's mingling gore enriches.
Rome ! although thy wall may perish,
Such manure thy fields will cherish,
Making gay the harvest-home ;
But thy hearths, alas ! oh, Rome !—
Yet be Rome amidst thine anguish,
Fight as thou wast wont to vanquish !

Yet once more, ye old Penates !
Let not your quench'd hearths be Até's !
Yet again, ye shadowy heroes,
Yield not to these stranger Neros !
Though the son who slew his mother
Shed Rome's blood, he was your brother :
'Twas the Roman curb'd the Roman ;—
Brennus was a baffled foeman.
Yet again, ye saints and martyrs,
Rise ! for yours are holier charters !
Mighty gods of temples falling,
Yet in ruin still appalling !
Mightier founders of those altars,
True and Christian,—strike the assaulters !
Tiber ! Tiber ! let thy torrent
Show even nature's self abhorrent.
Let each breathing heart dilated
Turn, as doth the lion baited !

Q

Rome be crush'd to one wide tomb,
But be still the Roman's Rome

From THE SAME.—PART III.

Chorus of Peasants.

THE spring is come ; the violet's gone,
The first-born child of the early sun :
With us she is but a winter's flower,
The snow on the hills cannot blast her bower,
And she lifts up her dewy eye of blue
To the youngest sky of the self-same hue.

And when the spring comes with her host
Of flowers, that flower beloved the most
Shrinks from the crowd that may confuse
Her heavenly odour and virgin hues.

Pluck the others, but still remember
Their herald out of dim December—
The morning star of all the flowers,
The pledge of daylight's lengthen'd hours ;
Nor, midst the roses, e'er forget
The virgin, virgin violet.

Enter CÆSAR.

Cæs. (*singing*). The wars are all over,
  Our swords are all idle,
  The steed bites the bridle.
The casque's on the wall.
There's rest for the rover;
  But his armour is rusty,
  And the veteran grows crusty,
As he yawns in the hall.
  He drinks—but what's drinking?
  A mere pause from thinking!
No bugle awakes him with life-and-death call.

Chorus.

But the hound bayeth loudly,
  The boar's in the wood,
And the falcon longs proudly
  To spring from her hood:
On the wrist of the noble
  She sits like a crest,
And the air is in trouble
  With birds from their nest.

Cæs. Oh! shadow of glory!
  Dim image of war!

But the chase hath no story,
  Her hero no star,
Since Nimrod, the founder
  Of·empire and chase,
Who made the woods wonder
  And quake for their race.
When the lion was young,
  In the pride of his might,
Then 'twas sport for the strong
  To embrace him in fight ;
To go forth, with a pine
  For a spear, 'gainst the mammoth,
Or strike through the ravine
  At the foaming behemoth ;
While man was in stature
  As towers in our time,
The first-born of Nature,
  And, like her, sublime !

STANZAS FOR MUSIC.

THEY say that Hope is happiness;
  But genuine Love must prize the past,
And Memory wakes the thoughts that bless:
  They rose the first—they set the last;

And all that Memory loves the most
  Was once our only Hope to be,
And all that Hope adored and lost
  Hath melted into Memory.

Alas! it is delusion all:
  The future cheats us from afar,
Nor can we be what we recall,
  Nor dare we think on what we are.

ODE ON VENICE.

OH Venice ! Venice ! when thy marble walls
   Are level with the waters, there shall be
A cry of nations o'er thy sunken halls,
   A loud lament along the sweeping sea !
If I, a northern wanderer, weep for thee,
What should thy sons do ?—anything but weep :
And yet they only murmur in their sleep.
In contrast with their fathers—as the slime,
The dull green ooze of the receding deep,
Is with the dashing of the spring-tide foam
That drives the sailor shipless to his home,
Are they to those that were ; and thus they creep,
Crouching and crab-like, through their sapping streets.
Oh ! agony—that centuries should reap
No mellower harvest ! Thirteen hundred years
Of wealth and glory turn'd to dust and tears ;

And every monument the stranger meets,
Church, palace, pillar, as a mourner greets;
And even the Lion all subdued appears,
And the harsh sound of the barbarian drum,
With dull and daily dissonance, repeats
The echo of thy tyrant's voice along
The soft waves, once all musical to song,
That heaved beneath the moonlight with the throng
Of gondolas—and to the busy hum
Of cheerful creatures, whose most sinful deeds
Were but the overbeating of the heart,
And flow of too much happiness, which needs
The aid of age to turn its course apart
From the luxuriant and voluptuous flood
Of sweet sensations, battling with the blood.
But these are better than the gloomy errors,
The weeds of nations in their last decay,
When Vice walks forth with her unsoften'd terrors,
And Mirth is madness, and but smiles to slay;
And Hope is nothing but a false delay,
The sick man's lightning half an hour ere death,
When Faintness, the last mortal birth of Pain,
And apathy of limb, the dull beginning
Of the cold staggering race which Death is winning,
Steals vein by vein and pulse by pulse away;
Yet so relieving the o'er-tortured clay,

To him appears renewal of his breath,
And freedom the mere numbness of his chain ;
And then he talks of life, and how again
He feels his spirits soaring—albeit weak,
And of the fresher air, which he would seek :
And as he whispers knows not that he gasps,
That his thin finger feels not what it clasps,
And so the film comes o'er him, and the dizzy
Chamber swims round and round, and shadows busy,
At which he vainly catches, flit and gleam,
Till the last rattle chokes the strangled scream,
And all is ice and blackness,—and the earth
That which it was the moment ere our birth.

There is no hope for nations !—Search the page
   Of many thousand years—the daily scene,
The flow and ebb of each recurring age,
   The everlasting *to be* which *hath been*,
   Hath taught us nought, or little : still we lean
On things that rot beneath our weight, and wear
Our strength away in wrestling with the air :
For 'tis our nature strikes us down : the beasts
Slaughter'd in hourly hecatombs for feasts
Are of as high an order—they must go
Even where their driver goads them, though to
   slaughter.

Ye men, who pour your blood for kings as water,
What have they given your children in return?
A heritage of servitude and woes,
A blindfold bondage, where your hire is blows.
What! do not yet the red-hot plough-shares burn,
O'er which you stumble in a false ordeal,
And deem this proof of loyalty the *real;*
Kissing the hand that guides you to your scars,
And glorying as you tread the glowing bars?
All that your sires have left you, all that Time
Bequeaths of free, and History of sublime,
Spring from a different theme! Ye see and read,
Admire and sigh, and then succumb and bleed!
Save the few spirits who, despite of all,
And worse than all, the sudden crimes engender'd
By the down-thundering of the prison-wall,
And thirst to swallow the sweet waters tender'd,
Gushing from Freedom's fountains, when the crowd,
Madden'd with centuries of drought, are loud,
And trample on each other to obtain
The cup which brings oblivion of a chain
Heavy and sore, in which long yoked they plough'd
The sand,—or if there sprung the yellow grain,
'Twas not for them, their necks were too much bow'd,
And their dead palates chew'd the cud of pain:
Yes! the few spirits, who, despite of deeds

Which they abhor, confound not with the cause
Those momentary starts from Nature's laws,
Which, like the pestilence and earthquake, smite
But for a term, then pass, and leave the earth
With all her seasons to repair the blight
With a few summers, and again put forth
Cities and generations—fair, when free—
For, Tyranny, there blooms no bud for thee !

Glory and Empire ! once upon these towers
    With Freedom—godlike Triad ! how ye sate !
The league of mightiest nations, in those hours
    When Venice was an envy, might abate,
    But did not quench her spirit ; in her fate
All were enwrapp'd : the feasted monarchs knew
    And loved their hostess, nor could learn to hate,
Although they humbled—with the kingly few
The many felt, for from all days and climes
She was the voyager's worship ; even her crimes
Were of the softer order—born of Love,
She drank no blood, nor fatten'd on the dead,
But gladden'd where her harmless conquests spread ;
For these restored the Cross, that from above
Hallow'd her sheltering banners, which incessant
Flew between earth and the unholy Crescent,
Which, if it waned and dwindled, Earth may thank

The city it has clothed in chains, which clank
Now, creaking in the ears of those who owe
The name of Freedom to her glorious struggles ;
Yet she but shares with them a common woe,
And call'd the " kingdom " of a conquering foe,
But knows what all—and, most of all, *we* know—
With what set gilded terms a tyrant juggles !

The name of Commonwealth is past and gone
   O'er the three fractions of the groaning globe ;
Venice is crush'd, and Holland deigns to own
   A sceptre, and endures the purple robe ;
If the free Switzer yet bestrides alone
His chainless mountains, 'tis but for a time,
For tyranny of late is cunning grown,
And in its own good season tramples down
The sparkles of our ashes.   One great clime,
Whose vigorous offspring by dividing ocean
Are kept apart and nursed in the devotion
Of Freedom, which their fathers fought for, and
Bequeath'd—a heritage of heart and hand,
And proud distinction from each other land,
Whose sons must bow them at a monarch's motion,
As if his senseless sceptre were a wand
Full of the magic of exploded science—
Still one great clime, in full and free defiance,

Yet rears her crest, unconquer'd and sublime,
Above the far Atlantic !—She has taught
Her Esau-brethren that the haughty flag,
The floating fence of Albion's feebler crag,
May strike to those whose red right hands have bought
Rights cheaply earn'd with blood.   Still, still, for ever,
Better, though each man's life-blood were a river,
That it should flow, and overflow, than creep
Through thousand lazy channels in our veins,
Damm'd like the dull canal with locks and chains,
And moving, as a sick man in his sleep,
Three paces, and then faltering : better be
Where the extinguish'd Spartans still are free,
In their proud charnel of Thermopylæ,
Than stagnate in our marsh,—or o'er the deep
Fly, and one current to the ocean add,
One spirit to the souls our fathers had,
One freeman more, America, to thee !

STANZAS TO THE PO.

RIVER, that rollest by the ancient walls,
  Where dwells the lady of my love, when she
Walks by thy brink, and there perchance recalls
  A faint and fleeting memory of me ;

What if thy deep and ample stream should be
  A mirror of my heart, where she may read
The thousand thoughts I now betray to thee,
  Wild as thy wave, and headlong as thy speed !

What do I say—a mirror of my heart ?
  Are not thy waters sweeping, dark, and strong ?
Such as my feelings were and are, thou art ;
  And such as thou art were my passions long.

Time may have somewhat tamed them,—not for ever;
  Thou overflow'st thy banks, and not for aye
Thy bosom overboils, congenial river !
  Thy floods subside, and mine have sunk away:

But left long wrecks behind, and now again,
  Borne on our old unchanged career, we move :
Thou tendest wildly onwards to the main,
  And I—to loving *one* I should not love.

The current I behold will sweep beneath
  Her native walls, and murmur at her feet ;
Her eyes will look on thee, when she shall breathe
  The twilight air, unharm'd by summer's heat.

She will look on thee,—I have look'd on thee,
  Full of that thought : and, from that moment, ne'er
Thy waters could I dream of, name, or see,
  Without the inseparable sigh for her !

Her bright eyes will be imaged in thy stream,
  Yes ! they will meet the wave I gaze on now :
Mine cannot witness, even in a dream,
  That happy wave repass me in its flow !

The wave that bears my tears returns no more :
  Will she return by whom that wave shall sweep ?—
Both tread thy banks, both wander on thy shore,
  I by thy source, she by the dark-blue deep.

But that which keepeth us apart is not
  Distance, nor depth of wave, nor space of earth,
But the distraction of a various lot,
  As various as the climates of our birth.

A stranger loves the lady of the land,
  Born far beyond the mountains, but his blood
Is all meridian, as if never fann'd
  By the black wind that chills the polar flood.

My blood is all meridian ; were it not,
  I had not left my clime, nor should I be,
In spite of tortures ne'er to be forgot,
  A slave again of love,—at least of thee.

'Tis vain to struggle—let me perish young—
  Live as I lived, and love as I have loved ;
To dust if I return, from dust I sprung,
  And then, at least, my heart can ne'er be moved.

STANZAS.

COULD Love for ever
Run like a river,
And Time's endeavour
　　Be tried in vain—
No other pleasure
With this could measure ;
And like a treasure
　　We'd hug the chain.
But since our sighing
Ends not in dying,
And, form'd for flying,
　　Love plumes his wing ;
Then for this reason
Let's love a season ;
But let that season be only Spring.

When lovers parted
Feel broken-hearted,
And, all hopes thwarted,
  Expect to die ;
A few years older,
Ah ! how much colder
They might behold her
  For whom they sigh !
When link'd together,
In every weather,
They pluck Love's feather
  From out his wing—
He'll stay for ever,
But sadly shiver
Without his plumage, when past the Spring.

R.

ON THIS DAY I COMPLETE MY THIRTY-SIXTH YEAR.

MISSOLONGHI, *Jan.* 22, 1824.

'TIS time this heart should be unmoved,
    Since others it hath ceased to move:
Yet, though I cannot be beloved,
        Still let me love!

My days are in the yellow leaf;
    The flowers and fruits of love are gone;
The worm, the canker, and the grief
        Are mine alone!

The fire that on my bosom preys
    Is lone as some volcanic isle;
No torch is kindled at its blaze—
        A funeral pile.

The hope, the fear, the jealous care,
    The exalted portion of the pain
And power of love, I cannot share,
    But wear the chain.

But 'tis not thus—and 'tis not here—
    Such thoughts should shake my soul, nor now,
Where glory decks the hero's bier,
    Or binds his brow.

The sword, the banner, and the field,
    Glory and Greece, around me see !
The Spartan, borne upon his shield,
    Was not more free.

Awake ! (not Greece—she *is* awake !)
    Awake, my spirit ! Think through whom
Thy life-blood tracks its parent lake,
    And then strike home !

Tread those reviving passions down,
    Unworthy manhood !—unto thee
Indifferent should the smile or frown
    Of beauty be.

If thou regrett'st thy youth, why live ?
    The land of honourable death
Is here :—up to the field, and give
    Away thy breath !

Seek out—less often sought than found—
A soldier's grave, for thee the best;
Then look around, and choose thy ground,
And take thy rest.

THE END.

BRADBURY, EVANS, AND CO., PRINTERS, WHITEFRIARS.

www.ingramcontent.com/pod-product-compliance
Lightning Source LLC
Chambersburg PA
CBHW020339030726
47496CB00007B/1941